Also by the Author

The Platinum Briefcase

Too Close For Comfort

CLOSE
ENOUGH

sands press
Brockville, Ontario

CLOSE ENOUGH

Henry Cline

sands press

sands press

A Division of 10361976 Canada Inc.
300 Central Avenue West
Brockville, Ontario
K6V 5V2

Toll Free 1-800-563-0911 or 613-345-2687
http://www.sandspress.com

ISBN 978-1-988281-57-5
Copyright © 2018 Henry Cline
All Rights Reserved

Cover Design by Kristine Barker and Wendy Treverton
Edited by Alyssa Owen
Formatting by Renee Hare
Publisher Kristine Barker

For information on bulk purchases of this book or any book published by Sands Press, please call 1-800-563-0911.

1st Printing November 2018

To book an author for your live event, please call: 1-800-563-0911

Sands Press is a literary publisher interested in new and established authors wishing to develop and market their product. For more information please visit our website at www. sandspress.com.

Dedicated to all the loving fans of Too Close for Comfort; I hope you enjoy this follow up to Jack's story...

Prologue

It's a feeling I really can't describe all too well. I know it's an "old" feeling: something primitive, something possibly sacred, but then again, I don't know anything for sure. I put "old" to symbolize that I know I'm only nineteen, but this feeling seems to transcend in nature. It's a want; it's a desire; and it's the only reason I ended up in yet another strange situation.

What's this old feeling that I'm talking about? The overwhelming desire for the truth.

Chapter One

Before you say anything, I have a feeling I know what you're thinking.

"What? There's more to this story? How is that possible?"

Here's my response: If you're talking about the story of Sam Miller and how his murder changed Stanton, Michigan, forever, I'd say, "No, you're right; that story is done". Of course, I always catch myself thinking about Sam, and I think about how Billy Young tricked Sam into killing himself, and I think about how Donovan Young cleaned up the mess to try and protect his cousin. (If you don't know that story, then suffice to say, I just ruined it for you).

But if you're talking about my story—Jack Sampson's story, then no, it's not over. I'm still breathing. There's still more that can be heard that is worth the time of day to listen to. At least, I think it's worth hearing.

But before I can tell that story (and I'd really like to), we'll need to bring you up to speed on a few things...

*****

Man, where do I even begin? There's a lot that needs to be said. Well, I think I left off on graduation night. Yeah... graduation night. What a night. Not only did I graduate from high school, but I also rekindled my romantic relationship with Alyssa Jackson. Not in a way that would make my mom worry about any imminent children, though. Just in a "Hey, you wanna be my girlfriend?" kind of way.

After the graduation ceremony and the reestablishment of our relationship, our school mentioned yet again that they'd be hosting a "lock-in" event at the high school and all the seniors were supposed to and urged to go. It was to ensure that kids weren't going around drinking and driving after graduation. I didn't want to go, even though my mom had already signed me up way early on in the school year and paid the fifty or so dollars to have me go. But once Alyssa tugged my arm for a bit, along with Emily Harper, and Ben Whey, and Douglas Floyd, and Harold Vero, and Mark Collins, and even Nick Wallace... Do you get the idea of how many people said I should go?

So as we played games, hung out, and drank some regular punch all night long at the high school, Alyssa and I held each other close and made sure to stay together as much as we could.

"Jack, this feels... like we never even broke up," Alyssa said with a luminous smile.

"I feel the same, Alyssa."

Once our group stopped groaning about our cheesiness, Principal Leonard made an announcement in the gym.

"Okay, everyone listen up... Yeah, even you, Gregory! The time is now 2 a.m., and I am tired. I know you kids stay up watching God knows what until the sun comes up the next morning, but we're going to start shutting down the games and turning off the lights. We have sleeping bags in the lunchroom for everyone, and I say 'for everyone,' as in, no one gets to share a sleeping bag. You can sleep near someone else if you're afraid of the dark, but don't share a sleeping bag. I can't stress that enough. Some of the other chaperones will be on patrol till your parents get you at nine a.m. So let's try to get a little shut-eye before that happens, shall we?"

Alyssa and I took Principal Leonard's advice and didn't share a sleeping bag—but we sure as hell pushed ours next to one another.

I put my right arm under her neck and her head rested on my shoulder. It was comforting, it was soothing...

"Hey, you better not fall asleep on me, yet," Alyssa said.

I started to yawn and shook my head side-to-side.

"No, no, I'm good."

"Sure."

Our eyes gazed through the floor-to-ceiling windows in the lunchroom as the night continued to consume our small town. Fireflies danced to each blade of grass as the moon peeked over the trees that engulfed us. The stars were out, along with the moon, and they were all shining bright enough to light the lunch room for the chaperones.

I felt warm and safe, and I could only hope Alyssa felt the same. But, there was one conversation that we hadn't had yet.

"Jack..."

"Yeah?"

"What a terrible time to get back together..."

I knew she was talking about going to college without me. She had mentioned after the graduation ceremony to my mom that she and Emily were accepted into an arts school just outside of North Chicago.

"Don't say that. I thought about that even before I asked you out."

4

"Really?"

"Yeah. We can make it work. I know we can."

"But, Jack...what are you going to do?"

The truth was, at that moment, I had no idea. Alyssa and I had talked about it before at the diner when we were trying to figure out Sam's death, but I hadn't given it any more thought.

"I thought about just taking a year off... maybe collecting my thoughts and trying to figure out something better."

Alyssa took her head off of my shoulder and stared deep into my eyes.

"Jack, I know you're upset about Sam, but he would want you to move on. He'd want you to go out and do something, not just sit around for an entire year."

I wanted to say her words were harsh since they did make me testy, but in the end, it was exactly what I needed to hear. She was right.

"You're right," I said. "There was one college that I was planning on going to, but they didn't have a football team so I threw it out as an option because Sam and I were going to go together."

"What would you go there for?" Alyssa asked.

I hated to shrug, but I did it anyway.

"I don't know, a business degree?"

"That's not a bad option, but..."

Alyssa's disapproval bothered me and I glanced away for a second. She, in a loving way, put her hand on my jaw and brought my head back to face her. My face was a little smooshed in her hand and she laughed. I couldn't help but laugh too.

"Cheer up, Jack Sampson. Everything will get better."

She came in to kiss me, but a chaperone didn't let us have much time.

"Okay, okay, okay, you two, cut that out. I don't want to have to stand over here all night."

Alyssa pulled her head back and we started to fall asleep. Or at least, that's what we let the chaperone think.

At 9 a.m., the Principal let the bell ring in the school and it was like waking up to a new nightmare. I never knew how weird it'd be to hear that sound for the very last time.

So, the other eighty-something bed-headed kids and I strolled out of the high school in a daze and got into our parents' cars. But just as I started climbing into my mom's car, she pointed and said, "Jack, it's Chief Ramzorin."

"What..." I said, still in a daze, "You said the Chinese are mowing?"

When I turned around and realized I was just being a tired idiot, I reached out my hand to shake the chief's.

"Good morning, Jack. Looks like you had a rough night."

"Yeah, well, sleeping on the lunchroom floor with an old smell of meatloaf wafting through the air can make your night a little restless," I replied.

Chief Ramzorin said, "Hah! I can only imagine."

"So, what brings you to the high school on this beautiful May 31st?"

"Well, now that I see you're mildly sleep deprived, how about you come by the station at 3 p.m.?"

"Is sleep deprivation a crime now?"

"Well, in certain cases it's worse to drive while sleep deprived rather than being drunk."

"You hear that, Mom?"

"Jack, stop clowning around," my mom scolded.

"Just, come by the station when you can—3 p.m. would be the best time for me. Mrs. Sampson, you can come too if you'd like. In fact, I'd prefer that."

Without either of us questioning any further, I took off my clown nose and climbed into my mom's car.

She asked the usual questions about how the night was, but she also knew I was drained. Although we didn't talk much, she said enough to keep me awake during the drive. But as soon as we were home, I took a power nap until one, hopped in the shower and got all cleaned up, ate lunch with my mom, and then we headed out to the police station.

"What do you think he wants to say?" my mom asked.

"I don't think he just wants to say something... I mean, he could've said it right then at the school," I replied.

"Not with how you were acting."

"Was I really that bad?"

"It was just annoying."

"Okay, thanks, Mom."

We shared a laugh and I texted Alyssa about going to the police station. She replied, "Okay, Detective Sampson" along with a tongue face emoji.

Once we parked in a good spot, we made our way in and Cheryl at the front pointed us towards Chief Ramzorin's office. When we walked across the center of the office, I looked over at Donovan's office and saw it was dark and the blinds were shut. A weird chill went down my spine and a flurry of memories shook me to my core. Was family really that important to him that he would cover up his cousin's murder of my best friend? But, I was launched back into reality when my mom asked, "Isn't that Mr. and Mrs. Miller in the chief's office?"

I automatically wanted to tell my mom that she must be imagining things, but when I looked through the glass wall, I saw she was telling the truth.

Sam's parents sat with their backs to us. When my mom and I neared the office, Chief Ramzorin waved us in and we opened the door.

Mr. and Mrs. Miller stood up and motioned to their seats as we entered.

"Jack, it's so good to see you, as usual," Mrs. Miller said with a faint smile.

"Hi Mr. and Mrs. Miller," I said.

Mr. Miller shook my hand and motioned again for me to sit where he'd been. Mrs. Miller hugged my mom and had her sit beside me. Chief Ramzorin remained sitting and also wore a faint smile.

"Well, I'm hoping that since none of you look unhappy, this isn't bad news," I said.

Chief Ramzorin let out a sigh and then said, "No, Jack, this isn't bad news."

"Okay," I replied.

Chief Ramzorin let his smile fade as he said, "Jack, what you did for Sam, what you did for his parents, for this community, we can never thank you enough. If it wasn't for you…"

"Well, Ben Whey had mentioned the idea that Sam was killed and didn't commit suicide; other kids who learned about my investigation gave their two cents as well. Along with Mrs. Miller, here."

"No," Mrs. Miller argued. "I was scared. I was in disarray. If it wasn't for your courage, Jack, I don't know that I would've ever mentioned Billy Young's name ever again. I had almost forgotten about him possibly being there until you rattled my brain with the theory that someone may have killed Sam, or led him to his death. And, I remember telling Donovan that I thought Billy was at the house with Sam when he did it, but Donovan denied it."

"It was a high stress and manipulated situation; we don't blame you, Mrs. Miller," Chief Ramzorin clarified.

"Look, I appreciate what you all are saying, but I've heard it enough times before. I just did what I thought was right," I explained.

"Yes, you did," Mr. Miller said, "Which is why we want to help pay for your college education."

"What?" my mom and I cried, blurting out our surprise in unison like a cheesy family film.

"You heard me," Mr. Miller said.

"No, you don't have to do that," I said.

"No, we don't have to by any means. But we want to."

"They want to use the money they had saved up for Sam to help you go to college," Chief Ramzorin said.

"We were going to spoil Sam. We knew he had the scholarships to play at a number of universities, but we were going to make sure he had plenty of money so he could focus on school and sports," Mrs. Miller explained.

"Mr. and Mrs. Miller, there's no way that we could…"

"Amanda, please, no matter what, we are going to give Jack this opportunity. He deserves it," Mr. Miller argued with my mom.

I knew he was serious. I mean, that's the only time adults seem to bust out the first name basis.

"I… I don't know what to say," I replied.

"Well, 'Thank you' would be a good start," Chief Ramzorin said.

"Yes, of course, thank you, a million times, thank you," I said as I turned to Sam's parents. They both smiled and I knew they believed in me.

"Thank you both, so much…" my mom said, and I thought she was going to cry.

I patted her shoulder and said, "Now, no offense Chief, but why did we need to have this discussion here, with you? Did you think it was going to get out of hand?"

"No, not really. I was going to ask what you wanted to pursue in college?"

"Uh…" I said, reflecting on how Alyssa reacted to my answer.

"Don't say a business degree or geology," Mr. Miller said.

Dammit.

"Jack, I think you need to pursue a degree in criminal justice."

And that's what ended up happening. With the money we saved from the survivor's funds after my father passed, along with the money from the Millers, I enrolled in a private college just north of Stanton, where I started my path to a criminal justice degree. Alyssa and I stayed committed to one another over the first year of college, making sure to go back to Stanton on our breaks and spend time together, and we would Skype each other on the weekends when we could. And it wasn't until the end of that first year, right when finals started, that Ben Whey started a group chat on Facebook to invite everyone to a get-together.

"Yeah, it's going to be in Stanton. Everyone that we graduated with is going to be there," Ben messaged.

I replied, "So, I don't get to wait seven more years to see your face again?"

"Haha," Ben said. "C'mon, Jack, it'll be fun. Mr. Saitov wants to host it at his bowling alley."

"I'm not opposed to going," I said.

"Oh, Jack, my car is only good for local travel," Emily said with a sad face at the end of her text.

"That sucks."

"Alyssa talked to your mom and your mom said for you to come out and get us."

"My mom wants me to drive five hours to Chicago to get you gals?"

"Yes, she wants to make sure we get there safe, I guess. Plus we don't have the money for a plane ticket."

"You could always take the bus."

Alyssa joined in on the conversation and said, "Babe, you're going to come get us. I don't care if buses have Wi-Fi, they smell."

"Okay, well my last exam is Tuesday and they want me out by Wednesday. When should I get you?"

"You can live in the dorms year round, but we would like to be out by Friday. So I'd suggest you go home, rest up, and then drive out Friday. Then the get-together is on Saturday, right Ben?"

"Yes, that's right."

"Okay, then it's settled."

The idea of having a gathering with everyone from high school was a nice thought and all, but I couldn't really imagine what it would be like after not seeing any of them for a year. Sure, I had seen them on Facebook or wherever else, but not in person, not by passing by them in the halls, and not by almost running them over in the school parking lot.

But when I called my mom, I found out it had been decided. My mission was to go to northern Chicago and pick up the precious cargo so we could all go to the party Saturday.

Sounds simple enough, *right?*

Chapter Two

Friday, May 24th, 2013

"Okay, Jack, don't forget to take a break if you need to when you're driving there," my mom said as I started to head out the front door.

"I'm not worried about my drive there; I'm more worried about the grades I made on my finals," I replied.

"Hopefully the Miller's money won't go to waste."

"No, I wouldn't let it."

She smiled.

"I know you wouldn't."

My mom and I hugged one last time and she said, "Just be careful, Jack. And bring those girls back safe. Party is tomorrow evening."

"Yeah, don't worry. Wouldn't want to miss it."

She kissed my forehead, something she hadn't done since I left for college. I looked at her for just a few more seconds with a smile before I parted from her and hit the road.

The drive to the north side of Chicago wasn't too bad. It wasn't the longest that I had driven in my life, but it still felt long. Having some music shuffling around on the radio made it a better experience. And, of course, I was pretty googly eyed every time I saw a dog in a car parallel to me.

The one stop I made didn't last too long. I was so excited to see Alyssa that I didn't want to waste too much time. And, sure, I guess I was excited to see Emily too.

Just kidding. Of course I wanted to see the both of them. Mainly Alyssa, though—just being honest. Y'know, since she's my girlfriend and all.

It was a lovely drive with mostly fields and older farmhouses. Well, that was the scenery until I drove through Chicago. Now that was cool.

When I first entered Eddington, it didn't look like a very artsy town. Most of the houses were a bit run down, kids left their bikes and outside toys strewn out in the front lawns. Then suddenly, like a difference between day and night, I entered the downtown area in the northwest region of Eddington. The buildings there were also obviously old, but everyone walking around was sharply dressed and living on their parent's credit card. Random shops and restaurants flooded the downtown area, most of them appearing to be expensive or for a certain clique. But when the GPS on my phone started acting screwy, I knew I was there.

About twenty miles from the state line of Wisconsin, I found myself at Eddington University. The sign that welcomed me was in the middle of a circular drive and I made my way past it. As I pulled into the parking lot that went around the entire school, I looked to see if Alyssa was anywhere to be found. The freshly cut grass was lush and green, and some students lay out in the sun after a long day of finals. I felt their pain. I really did.

The school was rather plain looking. It was built in the '60s and kept trying to stand the test of time, but a massive remodeling was in its near future. I could feel it. When I entered, there was one large brown building that appeared to be the administrative building. As I looked over the school, it appeared there was the main building in the north, three buildings in the middle, and two buildings at the south end, all connected together with catwalks, and from a sky view probably looked like a very large fellow. The buildings stretched out as much as they could without messing with the parking lot, and trees grew between the buildings and on the outside of the catwalks. I had a feeling the living quarters were towards the south end, so I started making my way towards them.

Finally, I felt my phone buzz in the passenger's seat and I slowed down in my black '99 Impala so I could check it.

The message was from Alyssa and it read, "You could have just told me you're here rather than driving around like a twelve-year-old."

Oh, Alyssa, so poetic.

I smiled and tried looking out the front windshield to see where she was. *Don't let her find you first, don't let her find you first…*

"Jack! Over here!"

"Dammit," I said unnecessarily as I saw her waving up ahead.

She was smiling and looked great as usual in a wavy blouse with dark jeans on. Her hair was still long but half of it was braided in a strange way (of course I mean a good kind of strange). But with that smile, I knew she was the same old Alyssa that I had seen on spring break and that I started liking back in junior year of high school.

As soon as a few bewildered students stepped out from in front of my car, I pulled into a parking space and shut off the engine. She didn't run towards me until I stepped out and made it at least six feet from the hood.

Then, she came running at me with all her might and I felt my heart rush with excitement.

Our arms wrapped around each other in an instant and I smiled. She was great, and I didn't want to let her go. But I knew we had to at some point. Otherwise, we'd be outside of her school all day, and Emily would get annoyed.

"Hi there," I said, and she backed away from me to give me a quick kiss.

"Heya, handsome. What brings you out this way?"

"Oh, I think you know why."

"Is it for the Stanton Ball, perhaps?"

"Well, it is at a bowling alley."

Alyssa made a face and replied, "Jack, you're supposed to play along."

"Oh, yeah…I mean, here's a glass slipper."

"Shut up."

She never sounded mean, just playful and loving. I didn't know how she could do it.

"I'd love to head right out of here, but I left my stuff up in my dorm. Can you help me with it?"

"Of course," I replied. "What kind of boyfriend would I be if I didn't?"

"The boring and usual kind," Alyssa responded.

We started walking towards the college to some entryway and I asked, "So if I'm not usual, would that make me unusual?"

"More like special."

"Sure."

She led me into the side door of one building and I stepped into a large lounging area. There was only a handful of students still hanging around, trying to study for whatever was next to come their way.

"Some of these kids don't go home on breaks. They just stay here," Alyssa explained.

"Is that allowed?" I asked.

"Yeah, didn't I explain in the group chat? As long as you're enrolled, you can stay here as much as you want. They actually have a special program for kids who were orphaned at a young age."

"That's good of them."

Alyssa guided me up the old staircase and across the walkway on the west side of the building. The windows had the sun peering through for plenty of natural light. No blinds of any kind on them. They also appeared to be fairly clean, along with the rest of the campus. Inside and out, the place appeared to be in better condition than the school I went to. But, not trying to compete or anything, maybe I'm just a little jealous. Plus, with as old as the exterior appeared, I thought it'd be falling apart.

After we walked by all the windows and a few hidden offices, we took the first catwalk to continue heading southwest. Another catwalk was parallel to the one we were currently in, and I wondered if any drunken idiots had waved to each other from either side. I would say they might have mooned each other, but it seemed that the students here kept their heads level, based on the lack of crazy stories Alyssa had for me.

"I assume you know where you're going," I commented as I glanced outside from the catwalk.

"Yes, somehow I know my way around the school I've been going to for the past nine months."

"Okay, just making sure, geez."

Alyssa scoffed and kept making her way over to where the dorms were. We passed by a few classrooms and labs and I was starting to feel a little bit of jet lag—well, car lag, if that's a term.

Finally, we made it through that building and started to walk through another catwalk. It was boring walking through the buildings, but I was just happy to be able to see Alyssa with my own two eyes, in person. The internet can be great and all, but I think the older generation knows what they're talking about when they say it's better to just meet and talk with people in person.

"Where's Emily?" I asked.

"I think she has to finish up some last-minute stuff with the dean of admissions."

"Is that a class?"

"Hah, no. It's her on-campus job. She was really lucky to get it."

"I'm sure she deserves it."

"I agree."

We finished walking through the catwalk and we were finally in the building with the dorm rooms scattered about.

"Southwest side is for women, southeast is for men."

"Not co-ed?"

"Definitely not."

Alyssa turned to me as she stepped up to her door and waited for me to stop. She had her hand on the doorknob and said, "But don't worry, I think you can drop in here for a second without much backlash."

"I would hope," I said, and I leaned in for another kiss.

Did I mention it was great to be with Alyssa again?

Anyway, once we exchanged a little bit of saliva, she turned the knob and revealed her room with a "Tah-Dah!"

It was a pretty plain room, with two twin beds that had matching sheets, a few posters here and there, a TV, one desk on each side, a clothing drawer on each side. Basically, everything in the room except the TV was mirrored.

"Well howdy doody."

"Do you like it?" she asked.

"Yeah, it's very… you and Emily -esque."

"Glad you think so."

Alyssa started picking her bags from off the ground but I reached in and helped her. I slung one over my shoulder and she grabbed her backpack and threw it over her shoulders.

"Should we make sure your bed works before we leave?"

Alyssa made a face and said, "Jack, stop."

I heard an annoying ringtone and Alyssa dug her phone out of her back pocket. Once she checked her text messages, she said, "Oh, it's Emily. She's ready for us."

"Do we have to walk back through the buildings again or is there a horizontal elevator?" I asked.

"No, we have to walk through the buildings again."

I let out an enormous sigh, but she didn't linger after the announcement was made. She made her way north to the complete opposite side of the campus. I'll spare the details of walking over there. And I wasn't out of shape or anything, just didn't care for all the walking after all of the driving I had done and would be doing again real soon.

Once we exited the final catwalk to the administrative building, we immediately turned left and I saw Emily leaning over, trying to pick up some files.

"Our ride is here," Alyssa said once we entered the glass door.

Emily stood at attention and I saw a smile run across her face. She was still as beautiful as ever, with thin and long blond hair and gorgeous eyes. (Wait, is that too much to say about the girl who *isn't* my girlfriend?) She had gained a few pounds since the last time I saw her, but who didn't? Also, she had grown an inch or two taller. She barely wore any makeup, but I knew she didn't need it anyway. Well, neither did Alyssa.

Whatever. I'll stop talking.

"Jack, it's so good to see you."

Emily came in for a hug and I accepted it, but she leaned in with her shoulders more than the rest of her body so it was clearly a friendly hug. She quickly parted from me and did a lame fist bump to Alyssa, which made them both laugh. I knew it would be a fun car ride back.

"I think you need to stop working. Isn't it summertime?" I asked.

"Well, yeah, but the dean wants these last files to be safely tucked away. This is important information, you know."

"What exactly is this?"

"This is the Dean of Admissions Office. If you could read, you would've seen it on the front of the door before you entered."

"Oh, I was distracted, I guess."

Alyssa rolled her eyes when she noticed I was looking at her when I said that and I laughed lightly. Emily rolled her eyes as well and said, "I'll be done soon, I promise. Donahue doesn't like to make me work late."

"Donahue? That's a majestic name," I said, and it sounds familiar...

"Something like that."

"No, I'd have to agree."

The clear and graceful voice came from out of our sight and I watched as a man stepped out from the hidden office on the left. He wore dark tan slacks and an off-white shirt with a very vibrant tie. His five o'clock shadow fit him well, but his receding hairline did not. He seemed like a nice man from the start, and I began to have a flash of memories that were trying to help me link him to my past.

"Mr. Donahue, you already know Alyssa, and this is..."

"Jack Sampson, yes!" Mr. Donahue said as opened his arms. "Do you remember me?"

Suddenly, all of the memories flooded in like a tsunami. Alyssa and Emily were visibly surprised as I hugged him and said, "Yes, duh!"

He patted me a few times on the back and we parted. He said, "How is your mom doing?"

"She's doing good, thanks."

"That's good to hear."

Stephen Donahue and I finished with our excitement and Alyssa and Emily were still surprised. I felt the same. I hadn't talked to him since my father's funeral, but he was a genuinely nice guy. My dad was friends with him in college and they'd tried to stay in contact, even when my dad was away on deployment. And I have to say, it's always nice to talk with someone who can bring me that much closer to the father I had lost. He was a great family friend, but I knew he needed to distance himself from us after my dad's death. It would've been a little weird if he just came out to see me and my mom.

"So, you're picking the girls up to go out to Stanton?" Stephen asked.

"Yes, that's the plan, anyway."

"Well, that sounds fun. Stanton is a nice little town. Nothing much ever happens there, does it?"

Emily made a face and I decided now wasn't the time to tell that story.

"Well hey, Jack, I'd like to hear more about what's been going on in your life. Would you want to go have dinner over at Mike's Grill? My treat? And the girls can come too, of course."

Alyssa and Emily seemed excited at the idea of food, and my stomach seemed to agree with them.

"Yeah, food sounds nourishing," I replied.

*****

Mike's Grill was right on the divide between the downtown area and the more run-down side. The grill was dark on the inside with heavy music playing, but it seemed to be a semi-family friendly restaurant. The food was good; I couldn't deny that. My burger was cooked just the way I ordered it and the fries were fresh and crisp on the outside. But the reason I say it was semi-family friendly is due to the fact that my burger was called The Annihilator; Emily had a gyro called the Wham, Bam, Thank You Lamb; and Alyssa had eaten a turkey sandwich called The Gobble, Gobble.

Once we finished our main courses, we went back to working on the chips and queso. Stephen was halfway through his second Stella when I wrapped up the story of what happened with Sam. I didn't want to tell it to him, but the "pursuing criminal justice" caught his interest, and Alyssa and Emily may have mentioned it as well at some point. It really sucks having a girlfriend who admires and cares about you.

"Wow!" Stephen exclaimed and I could smell the alcohol on his breath. "That's... that's crazy, Jack! And the Millers ended up paying for your college?"

"They said I deserved it—and that the money was for Sam's college fund—so why not give it to me?"

"That was extremely generous of them, but I agree with their decision. That's amazing. Jack, you're going places, I'm telling ya."

"Aw shucks," I said, feeling slightly embarrassed and awkward with his reaction. During my story, Emily never came in and talked about dating Sam, but I could understand why not. I took a drink of water to cool down and then I said calmly, "Thank you, I do appreciate it."

"Yeah, don't mention it."

Our waiter, who was only a few years older than us (excluding Stephen), came up and said, "I have the check right here, but did you guys want any brownie bangers to finish off your meal?"

If I have to hear one more stupid name of something on their menu...

Right as we all said, "No" to our waiter, Stephen's phone started buzzing violently from his inner coat pocket. He took the check in one hand and grabbed his phone with the other.

Stephen made a face as the initial notification turned into a phone call. "Excuse me, I guess I have to go back to my office and finish up one last thing."

My eye caught that the bill was around sixty dollars, so Stephen took out a money clip and placed four twenties on the receipt. Then he placed the leather book on the edge of the table and said, "Well, I'm really sorry that I have to run, but, when duty calls."

Stephen began to stand up and I could tell he was really in a hurry. He must've forgotten one last thing before he was able to enjoy his summer.

"Will you be okay to drive?" Alyssa asked.

"Yeah, thanks. I just had two. No big deal."

And just like that, he was out of the restaurant. He was in such a hurry, I saw him bump into the side of the bar on the way out. Emily and Alyssa didn't seem all that bothered by his actions.

"Mr. Donahue, always a strange guy," Emily said.

But since I was the one who was in the pursuit of a degree where nothing was as simple as it seemed, I started wondering why he was in such a hurry. Besides that he might be in a hurry to finish up this semester and sit on his ass for the rest of summer without dealing with applications from students and such, there had to be something else. He was so calm earlier, so why the big rush?

Alyssa could tell it bothered me and she asked, "Jack, are you alright?"

I decided to hide my suspicions by saying, "Yeah, maybe I had too much queso."

"Sorry, darling," Alyssa said and she patted my hand with hers.

I smiled and Emily suggested, "Well, should we stay here for the night? I mean, it's almost nine o'clock."

I checked my watch and saw that Emily was right. I didn't know if I could drive another five hours again unless I drank an energy drink. But I knew that wouldn't mix well with the rest of the food I had just consumed.

"Where would we stay? A hotel?" I asked.

"No, we could go back to the college," Alyssa said. "We don't have to be out of the dorms right away, or even at all. Like I said, some people stay there during the summer."

"Okay, then let's do that. Because I feel like any second now, this Annihilator burger is going to annihilate my asshole."

Emily made a face and said, "TMI, Jack."

Safe to say, I was the only one laughing as we left the restaurant.

*****

I had to say, the nightlife in downtown Eddington was on fire. Everyone was clawing away at every restaurant and bar in sight. All of those fancy people I mentioned earlier were out getting their party on. I was envious that they had a distraction. Because for the life of me, I couldn't shake the feeling that Stephen might be in danger.

We were getting closer to the university and I could tell Alyssa and Emily were excited about spending one last night in their dorms before they were able to return home to their bigger rooms. I really didn't want to assume that I'd be sleeping in the same bed as Alyssa, but I had done the math. There were two beds in the dorm room—and three of us—and two of us are dating, so...

Anyway, I was just glad that I didn't have to make the drive twice in one day. And I mean, I could have done the drive twice in one day, but after walking through The University of Long Walks, I felt it was time to get some rest. But as soon as I saw the blue and red lights flashing as we entered the parking lot, I knew it was still going to be a long night.

Chapter Three

The boys in blue were out in full swing as they tried locking down the crime scene. The yellow tape was being distributed to where the administrative building was completely closed off to the general public. It made me worry that whatever happened at the school had spread out in the entire building. And with as many school shootings as there seemed to be nowadays, my stomach really started twisting into a knot.

"Jack, park over there and let's see what's going on," Emily demanded.

"You got it."

I pulled over to the closest spot I could find that wasn't occupied by police cars or CSI vans and threw my car into park. Emily jumped out immediately and Alyssa called for her.

"Jesus, you don't think something happened to Donahue?" Alyssa asked.

"We're going to find out," I said as the thought crossed my mind.

Alyssa and I jumped out and slowly ran over to where Emily was, which was over by the crime scene tape arguing with an officer.

"Look, I can't let you past this line. This is a crime scene," the officer ordered firmly.

"Is Mr. Donahue okay? Mr. Stephen Donahue?" Emily asked frantically.

It wasn't hard to figure out Stephen's fate. The officer's face turned grave and Emily turned to hug Alyssa. As Alyssa tried her best to console her, I said, "We may have been the last ones to see him alive."

"Well, the detectives will definitely want to talk to the three of you," the officer said as he started speaking into his walkie.

I stepped back and turned my attention to poor Emily and the loving Alyssa. I hated to see Emily like this all over again. I know that she wasn't in a relationship with the man or anything, but they had worked together. Hell, I even started missing the guy the more I thought about it. He had been so kind and so caring to me and my family. Sure, we hadn't talked in a long time, but seeing him again just reminded me of all the good things he had done.

"Emily, I'm sorry," I said.

Before I could say any more, a new man appeared from the shadows of the parking lot and I noticed he was walking right towards us. He had a darker complexion of skin, but I couldn't tell what ethnicity he might be. He wore a plain black shirt, jeans, nice tennis shoes, and was well groomed. I was just about to say something, but Emily looked up and said, "Ammon!"

Emily released herself from Alyssa and bolted over to the mysterious man, who was about the same age as our waiter from before. Instead of staying blank-faced, Ammon started to look concerned as he saw Emily's reddened cheeks. He opened his arms and they hugged.

"Who is that?" I asked.

"Ammon Samara. He was Mr. Donahue's main assistant."

Did the news travel that fast?

I started eavesdropping on Emily and Ammon's conversation as I approached them.

"No… I can't believe it… he can't be dead."

Ammon's head titled up from staring into Emily's eyes to paying attention to me and Alyssa. His face was saddened as he said, "I was just coming up here to get something from his office that I had forgotten. Then I saw all the lights and…"

"We just ate with him at Mike's Grill not twenty minutes ago," Alyssa said.

"Did he say why he was coming here? I thought I had finished all of his work?" Ammon asked.

"No, he just grabbed his cell phone and rushed out of the restaurant. Didn't really say why."

Emily was still in his arms and she continued crying. He kissed her on the forehead and gave her one last hug before they parted.

"My name is Ammon, and you are?"

He was talking directly to me, so I replied, "Jack Sampson."

"Oh yes, Jack; I've heard about you from Emily and Alyssa."

We didn't shake hands. Instead, he did a sort of "courtesy nod" and I returned it. He seemed like a nice enough guy, but I started to wonder if he and Emily were more than friends. Either way was fine with me, but I needed to change some picture frame in my mind that still had her and Sam together.

"You said they're over here?" a loud female voice said from behind us.

I turned just in time to see the officer from before nod and point right over at us. The woman and her male counterpart made their way over to us and we all turned to them.

Time for more introductions…

"Hello, I'm Detective Flores, and this is Detective Hannigan with the EPD. We were hoping we could take you down to the station and start asking the four of you some questions."

I thought maybe Ammon would become uneasy or something, but instead, he said, "I'd be happy to answer any questions you may have, detectives."

"Good. Does that go for the rest of you?" Flores asked.

"I mean, do you want me to be a hassle and get a lawyer instead?" I asked.

Alyssa and, well, no one appreciated my joke and Flores said, "That's up to you."

"No, we'll comply," Alyssa said before I dug a deeper hole.

*****

About an hour later, I was sitting alone in an interrogation room that was nearly the same temperature as a walk-in fridge. There wasn't anything in my criminal justice classes that taught us the proper temperature for a questioning room, but I noticed that they all seemed to be cold, no matter where you were.

The detectives were nice enough to drive us over to the police station, but we were separated into different rooms once we arrived. I could hear faint murmuring from the other rooms, and I knew that I would be the last one interviewed.

Fortunately, that gave me some time to mull over the details leading up to Mr. Donahue's death. (Let's just call him Stephen, for consistency's sake.) He didn't necessarily seem concerned for his life when he left the restaurant. I mean, if I knew I was meeting with death, I don't think I would rush out of a restaurant before finishing the rest of the chips and queso. So, why did he leave so urgently? What was the message he received before he decided to run off?

I laughed lightly at the idea that it was someone texting him to say, "Hurry up and let me kill you, my show comes on at ten," but I knew it was in bad taste. He was a nice guy, an honest man. That's what I remembered my father saying about Stephen. And my mom had mentioned it when Stephen made his speech at my father's funeral. The more I thought about it, Stephen had been one of the best speakers out of anyone there. Personally, I was too afraid to speak. My mom had felt the same way. I regretted not saying anything at my dad's funeral, but it probably would've gone the same way that my speech did at Sam's funeral.

I missed my dad. I missed Sam. And now, I was really starting to miss Stephen.

Who would've killed him? And why?

Before I could answer my own questions, the two detectives Hannigan and Flores made their way into the room with me. I hoped their breathing would provide some sort of warmth to the room because their grim expressions weren't doing anything to help.

"Mr. Sampson, or should I call you, Jack?" Flores asked.

She was quite a beauty with plenty of hidden strength. Hannigan, not so much on the beauty side. Hannigan was the kind of guy that a girl married after she was done chasing all the members of her favorite '80s metal bands. He was black, had a bit of a gut, thick cheeks, but still seemed to work out his legs and arms. I wouldn't mess with him.

Flores dressed in a nice flowing blouse with a light jacket on over it. She had a bit of cleavage exposed, enough to keep a middle schooler guessing what was underneath. Her skin was a darker tone, almost olive, and her eyes were a creamy brown. Her hair was down earlier, but now she had it up in a messy bun. Neither of them had wedding rings, and neither of them seemed to care.

"Jack is fine with me," I replied, "As long as it's not followed by 'ass.'"

"Wouldn't dream of saying that," Hannigan replied smoothly.

I looked at both of them, trying to see who wanted to be the good cop and who wanted to be the bad one.

"So, as much as I would love to help, I feel like I wouldn't really be of much use."

"But you knew Mr. Donahue pretty well, correct?" Flores asked.

"He was a family friend. Spoke at my father's funeral."

"We're sorry to hear that," Flores replied. "How well did you know him?"

"Pretty well, but I hadn't seen him in a few years. I mean, I was young when I first met him, maybe seven or eight. My father died when I was fourteen, so that's when he stopped coming out as much. I may have seen him somewhere in between then and now, but I can't remember. And then… I saw him today."

"Emily worked alongside him. Is that true?" Flores asked.

Hannigan seemed to be relaxing in the background, waiting to see if I was going to be any trouble. I figured he wasn't just waiting for violent trouble, but even just a smart mouth.

"Yes, that's what she told me."

"And Alyssa, who I understand is your girlfriend, she knew him?"

"Didn't you already ask them these questions?"

"We're cross-verifying, but yes," Hannigan said.

I knew it. He was the look-out for a smart mouth.

"Well yes. Emily and Alyssa are roommates. They were friends in high school. We all were, actually, which is why I was here to pick them up and take them back to Stanton. Y'see, we come from a small town where we all like each other and share lawn equipment, and the owner of the bowling alley in our small town is going to have a little get-together for us since we've been out of high school for a year. Fun stuff, right? So when I got here to get the girls, Alyssa and I met up with Emily at around five-ish at the dean of admissions office, and Mr. Donahue popped out and said hello. Then he invited us all to Mike's Grill, which, by the way, has some of the stupidest names for their food items I've ever seen, and he ran off after getting a phone call."

"Seems like we don't even need to question you. You already know all the questions we're going to ask," Hannigan stated.

"Maybe not all of them, but something like that."

"Alyssa warned us that you were going to school for criminal justice. How's that working out for you?" Flores asked.

"Why? Are you needing my help in this case?"

"No, definitely not."

"I mean, your story lines up with what Miss Emily and Miss Alyssa were saying, so I don't see the point in questioning you further, unless you have any other leads for us?" Hannigan asked with a dryness that made me wish for a glass of water.

"Well I could ask you both some questions, if you don't mind."

"Like what?" Flores asked.

"Did Mr. Donahue have a wife? What did his last text message say, or who called him last? Has the video evidence been collected yet? What kind of murder weapon was used? And who are your next leads?"

"Good questions, Junior," Hannigan said. "We'll keep you updated. Or not."

"We have people looking into those items for us as we question the four of you."

I had forgotten about Ammon being brought up to the station in a separate squad car. Maybe he provided them with some insight.

"Y'know, I'm starting to get curious as to whether or not you have any ballistics training," Hannigan asked as he waved the folder at me.

"So he was shot?" I asked.

Hannigan and Flores knew I wouldn't let up, so they decided to give me a piece of the pie.

"Here, have a look for yourself."

It seemed unprofessional of Hannigan to just hand over the file like it was nothing, but I knew they'd do it for the next perp they grabbed as well. So, might as well hand it over to me.

In my second week of school, we had watched some video footage and seen pictures of dead people lying around in the streets and in offices and just about anywhere else you can imagine, but that didn't make it any easier for me. As much death as there was that surrounded me, I wasn't comfortable with it, and I hoped to never be completely immune to it.

Hannigan released the file once I had a grip on it and I placed it on the table. When it was flipped over, I saw several photos of Stephen at different angles. Stephen's final resting pose was him lying on the desk with his arms making a lousy diamond shape around his head. Blood was all over the desk. The two exit wounds on his back were jagged and I knew it was a higher caliber pistol, probably a forty-five ACP.

I vocalized my guess at the caliber and they both seemed happily surprised.

"You got it," Flores said.

"And he was shot face-to-face?"

"One of our CSI couldn't tell if Donahue had sat up for a second, was fired upon, and then fell over, or if there was some kind of confrontation before the pistol was discharged."

I glanced at the pictures one last time and then closed the file. I didn't need to see him dead.

"I can't imagine why anyone would want him dead. He was a nice guy, always had been."

"Bad people don't like nice guys, and we all know there's more bad than good out there," Flores poeticized.

"That's what they tell me," I replied.

Flores took one last look at me and said, "Well, I think we can let you and your friends go. If you have a party to attend, we don't want to make you late to it."

Hannigan and Flores made their way over to the exit and I stood up to walk with them.

"Thank you for your hospitality," I said as they opened the door.

"Don't mention it," Hannigan said.

Oddly enough, they closed the door behind me and left me out in the hallway by myself. But soon enough, I heard Alyssa's voice at the other end of it.

"Jack!"

Alyssa ran up to me as Emily and Ammon stayed behind at the end of the hallway. I took hold of Alyssa and we hugged for a few seconds. They seemed slightly phased, but not too upset. Interrogations were never easy, especially when the detectives were monotone and grim. Hannigan and Flores weren't too bad to me, but I had no idea what kind of experience the others might have had.

"Are you okay?" I asked as Alyssa stepped back from me and we locked eyes.

"Yeah, I'm fine."

We locked lips and then made our way over to Emily and Ammon.

"Ammon, I'm sorry for your loss as well," I said.

"I appreciate that, Jack, and know that I feel the same towards all of you."

I nodded and Emily gave me a small smile.

An officer came along and walked us out through the front of the small station. Once we stepped outside and heard the crickets chirping and the traffic dying down, Alyssa said, "They told us that we can head back out to Stanton. Is that what they told you?"

"Yeah, they said they didn't think they needed us anymore," I said. "We're no help."

"So, I guess we can head out to Stanton and be there by two or so?"

I stared at Alyssa for a second, and even if I'd chosen my next words very carefully, I knew she'd still be upset.

"I'm not in too big of a hurry to get back to Stanton," I replied.

"Oh, well, good idea. My grandparents will be asleep by the time we arrive. So, we could stay the night here and head out first thing in the morning."

"That's not really what I was thinking either, babe."

Alyssa gave me a look and then gave me the look.

"No, no, you're not saying what I think you're saying."

"Well, I haven't said anything yet, so technically…"

"Jack."

"Alyssa."

Her eyebrows furrowed as I said, "I want to stay here and do more investigating into why this happened, and who did it."

"But why? There are cops here who will take care of it. Trained professionals."

"Alyssa, I know that, but... I don't know, something isn't right about all of this."

Then, to my surprise, I had a supporter.

"Jack's right," Emily chimed in. "I think we should stay. We should stay and try to figure out what we can before we head out. There's no reason anyone would've killed him, and I want to know who and why."

Alyssa stood there with her hands on her hips, and Ammon felt compelled to say something.

"I mean, I live here, so I kinda have to stick around."

"Oh, shut up, Ammon."

"So, is that a yes?" I asked with a smile.

Alyssa looked me up and down, not excited at all for the journey ahead. But finally, she said, "Ammon, we're staying at your apartment."

Chapter Four

Saturday, May 25th, 2013

It was easy to tell my mom that we needed to stay the night in Eddington. I couldn't tell her the full truth, even though I trusted her. But I knew she wouldn't like the idea of how I was putting myself in harm's way, and sometimes I wasn't sure I liked the idea of it either. Even so, I was perplexed by the thought that someone hated Stephen so much that they'd killed him. Or was it even a crime of passion? Maybe Stephen got himself into some kind of trouble? I felt there was only one way to find out: my way.

We all stayed at Ammon's apartment for the night. He lived in a pretty swank studio on the corner of a fancy ass building in the downtown area. The complex even had underground parking, which is where he tucked away his nice BMW, and I shamefully parked my crappy Impala next to him. I didn't ask too many questions since we were his guests and I lived on borrowed money too, but he mentioned something about his parents sending money from Egypt to fund his lifestyle. Lucky.

Alyssa and I had slept on the floor next to each other, and I started thinking about how a year ago, we were doing the same thing in our high school. This time, there wasn't a strange smell of meatloaf or too many other kids around us, though. So I think we both slept a lot better than last time.

Once we were all awake, Ammon started making some cheesy scrambled eggs for us and had some peeled oranges on standby. We all fueled up and got ready for the day ahead.

"So," Ammon said as he took a triangular piece of toast and scooped up some eggs, "what's the big plan?"

Alyssa and Emily had their mouths full, so I made a suggestion.

"I was thinking we could go into the dean's office and see if we can find any clues. I know the police have probably ransacked the place, but it's possible they left something behind."

"Good thinking," Ammon said.

"Did you decide to call into work and come with us?" Emily asked.

27

Ammon smiled and said, "I would love to be a part of the Mystery Machine gang, but unfortunately, Harriet's Electronics needs someone to do their bookkeeping."

"You work at the school and at a store?" I asked.

"The school on the weekdays; the store on the weekends. The store lets me stay as little or as much as I want, though, so that's a nice perk. However, since it's the end of the month, I have a lot more than usual that I need to do."

I nodded and continued eating. The scrambled eggs were done just to my liking: not runny at all but not burnt in the slightest, either. Alyssa made a face at me once or twice and I barely kicked her under the table.

"By the way, I was going to leave this for all of you," Ammon said as he dug around in his jean's pocket and placed a key on the table. "Just in case staying at the campus sounds lousy."

"That's very kind of you, Ammon," I said.

"Please, I'm only doing what I think is right, just as you are. Donahue was my friend, too. I appreciate that you guys want to look into it further, and I want to help any way I can."

Ammon finished up his plate and took it over to the sink. He went ahead and rinsed it off and set it in the dishwasher.

"Guess I'll be heading out. Don't get in too much trouble."

Ammon made his way to the front door and I saw Emily finish up her plate quickly and meet him over at his door. They had a conversation in a low tone and I decided to ignore it.

"So you don't always eavesdrop on everything?" Alyssa asked.

"Only if it's pertinent to the case, or a hint to my Christmas presents," I replied as I finished my orange.

*****

The girls and I headed over to the college around noon and drove up to find most of the police tape was gone and the parking lot was practically empty. Only the skid marks from the night before remained, and I parked as close as I could to the curb to minimize the walking distance.

"Everyone cleared out after what happened," Alyssa said.

"I don't blame them. A haunted school isn't necessarily something I'd want to stick around for," I said as I turned off the engine and stepped out of the car.

My attempt at an unneeded joke was ignored and they followed me to the main building. The birds sang for us as we approached the school, but the song was a little too jolly for why we were there.

"Anything in particular that we want to look for, Jack?" Emily asked.

"Good question, Emily, and I'm glad you asked," I said, which is what I liked to say when I was still collecting my thoughts to their original question. "Anything the killer may have left behind, anything the dean left behind, anything anyone left behind that might link them to the killing, just anything out of the ordinary. And with you here, you know what the office should look like, so that helps a lot."

Emily smiled briefly and I hoped she was still holding up okay. Don't get me wrong, I was hurt by the loss of Stephen, but at the same time, I hadn't seen the man for a few years. Emily had been working with him every week during the school year, so I couldn't guess what her feelings were about the whole thing. Ammon seemed to be able to comfort her, though. I didn't plan on investigating their relationship any further. Come to think of it, I didn't know where Emily had ended up sleeping last night.

Ew.

As we approached the glass doors on the first floor, I let Alyssa open them and I cautiously stepped in. I worried that even though the tape was down, there would still be a few cops sticking around making sure no one was, well, doing what we were doing.

When we were all inside and had the door closed behind us Alyssa asked, "Not that I didn't think of this before, but is it illegal if we enter the crime scene?"

"I think so."

She made a face after I gave my honest answer, but I made my way up the stairs, not giving too much thought to the consequences that could erupt from our presence at the school. It's not that I didn't care, but, okay, maybe it was because I didn't care. Not in order to solve this case.

I turned back to Emily and Alyssa to make sure they were still with me, and I peeked over at the doorway. It was wide open, but the yellow crime scene tape was a flat "X" right in the middle of the doorway. Because of how they taped it, we could easily duck under and make our way into the office, which I did first.

"Watch your step," I said.

I covered my hand with the bottom of my shirt and turned the fluorescent lights on. The blinding light blinked overhead and then came on, exposing all the evidence markers that were left behind. The front area was a mess, and I wondered if it was the cops that had come through or a Tasmanian devil.

Anyone who had been on the scene had filled the trashcans with all their personal trash, the desks had drawers yanked open and messed with. Nothing was left untouched, except all the instruction manuals in the bookcases.

Emily gasped as she stepped in and said, "They really ripped apart my desk!"

"Yeah," I said, and I saw the dean's office doorway was wide open as well.

I walked on over to it and peeked in. Although the office was the same darkness as the other area was before I turned the light on, there was a deeper darkness to it that I couldn't explain. Maybe it was due to the fact that we knew what had happened there, and the massive permanent blood stain on the dean's desk left an unwritten epilogue that kept us all still guessing what really happened, and why.

There were two markings on the ground and I figured that's where the bullet shells had been before they were taken up for ballistics testing. If only I knew someone on the inside of this police station.

My next thought was the dean's computer. His monitor was still there, just collecting dust. But as I rounded the corner, I saw that they had definitely followed protocol.

"His CPU is gone," I said, cursing to myself.

"Mine is gone, too, along with Ammon's," Emily said from the front area.

"Well that takes away most of what I was hoping to find here," I said as I stepped back into the front area.

Emily seemed saddened as Alyssa said, "Aren't you forgetting the easiest piece of evidence we could look for?"

"Huh?"

"Security footage."

I replied, "Well duh, but we don't have a way to access that, do we?"

Alyssa smiled and said, "You may need to add this to your list of things you like about me."

We all made our way to the basement area of the main building that was a lot more hidden than it needed to be. The musty smell and stained concrete walls displayed the building's age, and I couldn't help but wonder if all the doors we passed in the odorous concrete hallway were just broom closets. Alyssa assured me that there was more to come, so I continued following her and Emily along the brightly lit basement. I didn't think Alyssa was just taking me for an underground tour, but I hoped that whatever she planned on showing me was actually attainable. Having security footage to watch and mull over would be great. Maybe then, we could see who the killer was.

But when Alyssa reached for the knob on the door labeled Authorized Personnel Only, she found that it was locked.

"I have a feeling we're not part of the 'Authorized Personnel,' so you don't have a key." I said.

Alyssa made a face and said, "No."

"Well, it was worth a try."

I started to walk off by myself, but there was a rattling from the door that caught my attention again. The oblong door handle swung up and down and the person on the other side was having quite a struggle getting it open. At last, the door popped open and a short, scrawny, red-haired and bearded man opened it.

"Lewis!" Alyssa said happily.

The man had a half-eaten sandwich in one hand and was pleasantly surprised to see Alyssa.

"Alyssa! I thought you had probably run off by now," he said with mayonnaise on his mustache.

He tried to give Alyssa a one-armed hug, but she signaled that he had something on his reddish-brown mustache and he said, "Oh, whoops."

He moved back from the door and we waltzed our way into the dimly lit room. There were all kinds of electronics all over the place: modems, routers, servers, computer screens, and a shit ton of wires all over the walls and up on the ceiling. It was the kind of room that you didn't want to have to change a single thing in, but I'm sure Lewis had to every once in a while.

Lewis stepped over to a computer desk where all eight of his monitors stared intensely back at him. I looked over each monitor and saw they were live feeds of the security footage around the campus, and then there was another monitor to his side that was used to control all the others. He grabbed a napkin rather slowly but wiped his face quickly. After he set his sandwich down on the table as well, he said, "So what's up? How's summer?"

"Well, technically it just started," Alyssa replied.

"Who are your friends? Oh, wait, I know Emily. But who's that guy with the big eyebrows?"

I don't have big eyebrows, do I?

"That's my boyfriend, Jack Sampson."

Lewis seemed disappointed that I was her boyfriend. Or maybe it was that he was in his forties and crammed in a computer room. Or because he had red hair. Who knows?

He brushed it off and said, "Well hey, Jack. You have yourself a nice lady."

"Thanks."

Next, we all decided to be completely silent and make the situation weird. It just happens sometimes I don't know why. All I could hear was the computers softly running and Lewis breathing.

"So, are we all hanging out?" Lewis asked.

"Not exactly. Sorry," Alyssa said. "We were hoping we could have a look at the footage."

"Oh! So you wanna see where that one kid fell on his face while skateboarding? That is a classic video; I still have it right here," Lewis said as he got all excited and started typing away at his keyboard.

"No," Alyssa said, seemingly annoyed, "whatever footage you may have given to the police last night."

Lewis glanced at each of us and didn't seem as thrilled as before.

"Oh, okay. Now I see why you're here."

He didn't seem sad, *per se*, but I guess he was hoping we were there to watch skateboarding fail videos with him.

"Mr. Donahue was a funny guy, did you know that? He had a different sense of humor, one you young'uns might not understand. Plus, some of it was kind of crass."

Emily seemed thrown off by Lewis' information as he pulled up whatever footage he could. Alyssa said, "No, didn't know that."

Lewis nodded and said, "Yeah, I kinda figured. He might have gotten in trouble if he told students some of the jokes he had."

"So, Lewis, what exactly do you do here?" I asked as nice as I could.

"Believe it or not, I'm a security guard. Mainly on the tech side, but I work here year round to make sure everything works the way it's supposed to and make sure no one messes with these wires."

Knew it.

Lewis finished typing and clicking all over the place and he said, "Okay, now the footage I handed to the police was hours and hours of footage, but I don't mind showing you this piece right here that I edited together. And I feel like it's what you're going to want to see."

His final words grabbed our attention and I leaned in towards the monitor even though I could already see just fine (y'know, for dramatic effect and all). Alyssa and Emily held their stance away from Lewis, but stared intently at the screen. In the scratchy footage, a figure appeared in all black clothing, a black hood over his head, black gloves, and the silenced pistol. It showed the figure step into the camera's view, which was really terrible. The camera must've been pointed almost directly down and adjacent to the office, only to where you could see someone walk in and out of the area where Emily and Ammon had worked, but not any of the catwalk doors. He entered without any hesitation, apparently determined to kill the dean. Before my imagination ran wild with what their confrontation may have looked like, the video cut to another camera feed that was at yet another terrible angle, but I'd take what I could get. It was above the other end of the catwalk, but pointed almost straight out instead of down. When I saw the very top of a door at the very bottom of the frame, I knew it was the bathroom door. And out walked...

"The janitor?" Alyssa asked.

The figure was now wearing a gray jumpsuit that didn't look very comfortable, and he held a duffle bag in his hands as he walked out of the school in the low lighting.

"Do you know the janitor as well as you know Lewis?" I asked Alyssa and Emily.

"Hey, maybe I know the janitor as much as I know Lewis," Lewis commented. I turned to him and his smile faded as he said, "Okay, not as well as I know myself, but if you think he's the one who killed the dean. I mean, he complained about his pay all the time but..."

"There's just no way, Jack. It doesn't make sense," Alyssa said, and Emily nodded.

"Even if it doesn't make sense, we should have a chat with him," I suggested. "I mean, he was here last night."

"Well, speak of the devil," Lewis said, and he pointed to one of the monitors that showed the janitor, in real time, mopping around the men's dorms.

Chapter Five

"Jack, I really don't think this is a good idea."

"Well, I don't think the design of this school was a very good idea."

We were making our way all across the campus to the dorms and Alyssa was arguing with me. I love the girl, but she has a fire that no one can extinguish.

"Okay, point made, but you didn't let us answer your question earlier."

Walking through the last catwalk before entering the dorm building, I said, "Oh, sorry, what question?"

"The one about knowing the janitor as well as Lewis."

"Oh yeah. Okay, so?"

"The answer is no."

"Any reason why?"

Emily finally chimed in.

"He's not very friendly, to say the least."

Not too threatened by her description, I went ahead and opened the doors to enter the building, and there he was, the janitor. Built like an ex-marine, he stood stout beside the rolling yellow mop bucket and gave us the thousand-yard stare. After receiving the look that made me want to pee myself, I said, "Hi, I'm Jack."

"Tim," he replied gruffly.

"Well hey, Tim, what are you up to?"

"Working," he replied and started mopping again.

He didn't talk like a giant, necessarily, but more like someone who was tired of talking, tired of fighting, tired of defending themselves. I couldn't blame him if he was feeling that way, especially as ex-military.

I glanced at Alyssa and Emily and Emily said, "Well, you've gotten him to talk a lot more than I ever have. I'd say keep going."

They remained in the doorway and I walked up to Tim, trying to look normal. But I knew my fear showed in every step that I took.

"So, uh, Tim, what kind of cleaning products do you use?"

"I know that's not why you're here to talk to me," Tim said, sounding irked. "I recognize the blond girl. You're all here about the dean. You've made your own Hardy Boys group."

"Yeah, something like that. Okay, well I'll cut right to it. Why are you still here?"

"It might be summer break for you and the two girls, but I've got until tomorrow to clean this place as much as I can, and then I can go on vacation."

"Where do you plan on going?"

"Wherever a kid isn't going to ask me stupid questions. That sounds like a nice start."

"Okay, now Tim, I tried to be nice in my approach, but you're not really reciprocating."

"I don't have to reciprocate. You assume that I killed the dean and I don't appreciate that gesture."

"I don't assume it, Tim. I just wanted to ask some questions."

"Well, looks like your time is up."

"Huh?" I asked. "No, I just got here."

To my dismay, Hannigan and Flores stepped past me to make their way towards Tim.

"Tim Davidson, Detectives Hannigan and Flores. We'd like to talk to you again, somewhere private."

"You're taking a custodian into custody?" I asked.

"Jack, you're hilarious," Flores said with such disdain, "but we have work to do."

Flores stepped away with Tim, and Hannigan stepped up to me, Alyssa, and Emily.

"Y'see, Jack, we don't really care for your continued involvement in this manner. And I'm sure Chief Ramzorin wouldn't like it either if you get what I'm saying."

I acted offended as I said, "Hannigan, you tattled?"

Hannigan wore a smug smile as he said, "Just get lost, and we won't have any other problems. I promise."

Hannigan stepped away after a raise of his eyebrows and disappeared with Flores and Tim. I turned around to face Alyssa and Emily, a little embarrassed by how things had gone.

"Jack, if they talked to Ramzorin, then that means…" Emily started.

"Don't worry, Ramzorin wouldn't run and tell our parents. Hell, I don't think Ramzorin even does much running anymore."

"I can't tell if you're making fun of his age or his weight," Alyssa said.

"Maybe I'm not ridiculing either one?"

We made our way back to my car and recognized our defeat. But it wouldn't be the last time we'd try to find the truth.

"How about I call Ramzorin so we can calm ourselves of any worry," I suggested.

"Sure. Emily, can we stop by the bathroom?"

"Yes."

"And I'll wait outside," I said as I looked up Stanton's Police Station on my phone and pressed the call button. The ringing began instantly and I felt a little nervous at how Chief Ramzorin would react.

"Stanton Police Station. This is Shelly."

"Hello, Shelly, this is Jack."

"The bird that flew the coop. I guess you wanna talk to the chief?"

"Please."

"Hold, please."

Shelly was a nice woman. She mainly stayed up at the front of the station for booking or to assist anyone coming in. I didn't know her name for a long time until everything with Sam happened.

Not that it never crossed my mind, because it did almost all of the time, but I couldn't believe that had happened only a year ago. It felt like forever since I had last seen Sam. Made me also wonder what was happening the last time I saw him, *or what were we doing? Was it that Friday after school?*

"Jack?"

I heard Chief Ramzorin's voice on the other end and I said, "Oh, hiya, Chief."

"Did you solve the case yet?" he asked.

"Haha, no. Working on it. But based on that question, I feel like you're on Team Sampson right now."

The chief laughed for a second, but then retreated a bit and said, "Jack, what you're doing is admirable. Really. And I know that Donahue was a family friend, but…"

"You think I should stop?" I asked, worried about what was going through Chief Ramzorin's head.

"I know if I tell you to, it won't do anything. You have the gift, Jack. I know you do. That undying perseverance," the chief slowed himself down. "If it can carry over to your future career as a detective, you'll be an amazing one."

I smiled. It was always good to get compliments from my future boss.

Well, unless he retired first. I would say that the Chief and I have a relationship that has evolved greatly since I first met him, but that's kind of obvious since he saved my life.

"Thank you, Chief."

"The only thing I need from you, Jack, is a promise."

"Well, I can't pinky promise you since we're on the phone."

"No, just a regular promise. Please be careful. You, Alyssa, and Emily. Whatever is going through your heads or whatever feelings are flowing around, just remember, you're chasing a killer. You're trying to find a *killer*. Their demeanor is not a theory, it is a fact. And I just want you to promise to be careful, okay?"

"Yes, of course, Chief. We'll all be careful. We can look after each other and ourselves."

"Good. Just," the chief sighed, building up to something unknown. "I never told you this story, but there was a kid, well, around your age. I used to watch him when I was younger. Tried keeping him safe. But he walked too far down the plank and I lost him. So, I don't want the same thing to happen to you—thirty... shit, almost forty years later."

It chilled me to hear Chief Ramzorin say he "lost" the kid. What did he mean? He had never mentioned this to me before, and I had a feeling he didn't tell a lot of people about it. I felt honored that he'd told me, and weird. But the warning was clear, and I was ready to keep the promise.

"I understand, Chief. And I promise, nothing bad will happen to us."

"Good, keep that promise. For me and for all of your parents."

"I plan on it."

"Good, because if you didn't, I was going to tell all your parents and get you guys in trouble."

"Yeah, please don't do that," I requested.

Chief Ramzorin laughed slightly to himself and I felt like he was ready to end the phone call. But, of course, I was wrong.

"Jack, there is one last thing I'd like to say before I let you go."

"What would that be?" I asked.

"Just remember—sometimes, two shaded figures can look very similar to one another, eh?"

I nodded and said, "Yeah, that makes sense," and we ended the call with our goodbyes.

Chapter Six

We all drove around the city and stayed in my ridiculously air-conditioned car to try and talk about what to do next. I know I don't like cold interrogation rooms, but a cold car is what's best for me.

"So, you're not giving up now, Jack, are you?" Emily asked.

"Pfft, no."

Alyssa rolled her eyes and Emily said, "Well, I feel bad that we're using so much of your gas. How about we stop somewhere to talk? Are either of you hungry?"

"I'm pretty hungry. Investigating crimes is a tiresome task," I admitted.

"I could eat something small," Alyssa said.

"How about Panera Bread?"

"Puh-what-uh bread?"

Emily pointed the way over to Panera Bread and we parked pretty close to the entrance. As we waited in line and I looked at the menu above the counters, I started to get a headache.

"Do you know what you want, Jack?" Alyssa asked. "I think that woman is ready to help us,"

"I don't know what most of this food is," I replied.

"Just get one of the paninis, c'mon."

Alyssa pushed me over to the cashier and I ordered something that sounded faintly phallic. Not as bad as the menu at Mike's Grill, but, you know. Alyssa got a half salad, and Emily ordered some soup and a grilled cheese. We split the payment into thirds, which seemed to irritate the cashier, but hey, only one of these girls is my girlfriend and even she declined my offer to pay for her.

The cashier handed over a flimsy metal number holder thingy and we carried it on over to the nearest table. Alyssa offered to fill my drink and hers, and Emily went along while I guarded the table. When they returned, we finally started talking.

"So, Tim the Friendly Janitor, guilty or not guilty?" I said as I took a sip of Coke.

Well, I thought it was Coke, but as soon as I made a face and turned to Alyssa, she said, "All they have is Pepsi."

"Okay, not the end of the world. So, guilty or not guilty?"

"Aren't you supposed to figure this out?" Emily asked. "You're the one wanting to be a detective."

"I mean, I don't have to include the two of you in this investigation if you don't want me to."

"Okay, I'll admit that came out meaner than I meant it to, but all I'm saying is, are you really going to listen to what we have to say even though we aren't as *experienced?*"

"Detectives don't have to be one hundred percent experienced. And besides, they talk to other people to form their opinions all the time. So, yes, of course I want to hear what you both have to say."

"Oh, okay," Emily said with a smile. "Well, no, as weird as Tim is... Weird is the wrong word—he's damaged—I could see it every time I've ever heard him talk. I can't see him killing Mr. Donahue."

"I agree," Alyssa said. "And if Tim was mad about his wages all the time, he wouldn't kill Mr. Donahue over it. He didn't set anyone's wages."

"What about you, Jack? What do you think?" Emily asked.

I didn't want to say anything since the waitress was coming up. Even though she didn't take our order, she seemed to know who ordered each item. The pauses between her announcements were filled with classical music that was playing overhead and bouncing off the lame green and orange walls. How delightful.

"Anything else for you?" the petite girl in a Panera ball cap asked.

Alyssa and Emily brushed her away with their words.

I felt the Panini burn my fingers the instant I touched it. So to let it cool, I shared my thoughts.

"No, it's definitely not Tim. As intense a man as he is, I don't think he'd kill Stephen, either. Now, for motive, I don't have anything on him, but frankly, I don't have anything on anyone when it comes to that. We'll have to do a lot more research before we can find some kind of motive. And forget about trying to find the murder weapon. That'll lead to unpleasantness and I promised the chief we'd be safe."

"I really don't know why anyone would kill Mr. Donahue, either. I mean, no one is perfect, but he was such a nice man. He had respectable friends, like your parents, Jack. I don't see him hanging around with crooks and thieves, and murderers."

Emily finished talking and diverted her suspended grilled cheese into the creamy red tomato soup. I nodded in agreement and so did Alyssa. We all decided it was time to take our first bites of food, so silence fell among us. My Panini was great, but I didn't notice that red onion was part of the ingredients. Oh well, not like I was allergic.

"I feel bad for Tim. I'm sure he really is a nice guy."

"Yeah," Alyssa agreed with me.

"Hopefully the detectives won't be too hard on him," I added.

"No. But that reminds me…"

Alyssa's face changed and she said, "I think what we're doing here is good, and mostly necessary, but I really don't want the detectives to call home and tell them what we're doing here. My grandparents would flip out."

"Yeah, Jack, I mean, I'd rather not go to jail. Ever."

"Oh, c'mon. They're not going to throw us in jail. We'll call this a friendly competition. Ramzorin knows that I'm not going to give this up, and I'm sure he told Flores and Hannigan that as well. It's not that I don't trust the detectives, because I do. I just, I want to solve this. I know I can, and I have a feeling that they're going to miss something. They're working more than one case right now, that's normal for them. But we can focus all our attention on this one case and close it ourselves."

Alyssa smiled and said, "I know we can do it, baby."

I smiled and said, "Thanks, love. I agree. But if it was just Flores, I would say we should run for the hills and go back to Stanton. On the other hand, Hannigan…"

"But Jack, isn't he the one who made the threat?" Emily asked as I neared the end of my meal.

"He's a competitor; I could see that the first time I talked to him. He likes me investigating parallel to them. Honestly, I should just call him up and ask what they found out."

"I dare you," Alyssa said deviously.

"Hell, I dare myself."

*****

"And who did you say you are?"

"Jack Sampson, I need to speak with Detective Hannigan if he's available."

"He's not on the phone, but he looks busy. Let me ask him."

What was the point in talking to Hannigan? I don't know. I really didn't think he'd reveal anything big to me before the media, but even if he told me that Tim was the wrong guy, that would help. But then what? How would we try to find the next person? What did we have to go on, besides nothing? The other good thing about calling Hannigan was that I could get a better read on if he would eventually throw us in the pen or not.

The silence on the other end of the line died and I started to say something, but Hannigan spoke first.

"Jack, of course you'd call."

Okay, Jack, don't screw this up. Just talk to the man.

"Well, of course you'd answer."

What a stupid thing to say.

"Actually, I am happy that you called because I wanted to know a thing or two."

"Like what?"

"Well, what did you talk to Mr. Davidson about?"

"He was just about to tell me a secret recipe for sugared rose petals, but then you guys interrupted."

"Haha. Look, Jack, it's been a long day and I still have a shit ton of work to do, so how about you cut it out and answer my questions, okay?"

Trying not to sound sad and scolded in my response, I said, "Okay, Hannigan, I understand."

"So what did you ask him?"

"In all seriousness, I asked what cleaning products he uses and why he was still at the school."

"Why the hell did you ask about the cleaning products?"

"I don't know. Are you mad that I did? Is it something you forgot to ask him?"

Hannigan laughed on the other end and said very plainly, "No."

"I asked him to try and break the ice, I guess. He is a pretty intimidating man."

"I see. And the 'why are you here' question. What was his response?"

"He said he had until tomorrow to clean the entire school and then he could start his vacation."

I heard the clicking of a pen at the other end of the phone. Not sure if it was the button at the top being pressed over and over or the clip on the side being retracted and released against the pen. It didn't matter which one he was specifically doing; it was annoying. Once he finally stopped, there was a sigh on his end and he said, "Man, Jack, I thought maybe you'd think of at least one thing that we didn't ask him."

"Most of my interrogation was spent with me frozen in fear at the sight of him."

"Still, after all the praise Chief Ramzorin gave you, I thought you'd ask some better questions."

"I'll be more prepared next time, trust me."

"If there is a next time," Hannigan growled. "Look, I know you're the small-town hero back home, but here? Flores and I investigate the crimes."

"I understand that. Just thought I'd be of some help."

"Not this time," Hannigan replied with a softened growl. His signals were so mixed. It was as if he threw them into a blender with a brand new blade.

"You're as confusing as my ninth grade girlfriend."

Hannigan was definitely smiling on the other end. He enjoyed the competition, just as I had predicted. I was flattered he considered me as a challenge.

"Tell you what, Jack, I will let you know this: Tim isn't our man. He has a video where he's in the bathroom during the crime."

"Saying the words 'video' and 'bathroom' in the same sentence makes me not want to watch it. Or do I?"

"It's not what your teenage mind thinks it is. Ever seen those rant videos on Facebook? I'm sure you have."

"Unfortunately."

"Yeah, well, look up Davidson the Angry Son and let me know what you think," Hannigan said, trying really hard not to laugh.

With a hard cringe, I replied, "Eh, I think I'll pass."

Hannigan pulled himself together and said, "Okay, Jack, is that all?"

"Yes, I think so. You've been a great help."

"Hah, wish I could say the same about you."

Hannigan hung up the phone. He'd had the last say.

Chapter Seven

Late Saturday Afternoon

We used the key Ammon had given us in the morning and went back to his apartment to rest and relax. Well, that was the plan for Emily and Alyssa. My plan was to rethink the entire thing.

"Ammon has Capri Sun? Really," Alyssa said as she dug in the fridge.

"Fine by me," I replied. "Sounds like you have a keeper, Emily."

Emily didn't seem too crazy about my assumption of their relationship, but I had a feeling about it.

"What are you blabbering about, Jack?"

"Oh, nothing, Mrs. Samara."

"Dear Lord, don't say that."

Alyssa gave me a look that said I should really cut it out, at least, with the silliness. So I went a more serious route.

"Okay, I won't. But if not a boyfriend, then are you just friends?"

Alyssa handed Emily a Capri Sun and closed the refrigerator door. I looked at both of them from across the wide-open apartment. They headed towards me from the kitchen and Emily said, "We worked alongside each other, Jack. That doesn't mean we have to be boyfriend and girlfriend. We just get along."

I didn't want to embarrass her about how I didn't know where she slept last night, so I wouldn't ask. Surely Alyssa knew plenty more than I did. And maybe I didn't want to know. Sometimes, I still saw Emily as Sam's girlfriend. Even after Sam was killed, even after Emily admitted that she had thought about ending things with Sam when school was over, I still saw her as Sam's girlfriend. But would I get mad if she was with someone else? No. I would just hope he was close to being as good as Sam.

"So, what's next, Detective Sampson?" Alyssa asked as she plopped next to me on the couch.

"I like Inspector, more."

"Of course you do."

Emily sat across from us and punctured her Capri Sun with the straw. I was happy to see she didn't seem too lonely or like a third wheel.

"Honestly, after speaking to Chief Ramzorin and Hannigan, I'm feeling conflicted."

"Conflicted on who could have done this or conflicted on staying?"

"The latter."

"Really? I thought you'd never give up, Jack," Emily said.

"I don't want to *give up*, I just feel like… I mean, with Sam's death, as soon as Ben suggested that it was murder instead of suicide, and the police denied it, I knew there was something more to the case. I felt it. But in this situation, I didn't know Stephen as well as I would have liked to after we lost contact with each other. And I'm not worried that Hannigan or Flores aren't fit to handle this case. I just… I don't know."

"Well in this case," Emily said, "I'm the one who's not convinced. Mr. Donahue didn't have any enemies. No one would have wanted to cause him harm. And the fact that someone did? That drives me insane. And as much as I want to believe that Hannigan and Flores are more than qualified to find who did this, I'd really feel better if we could find out first."

Alyssa tried to offer condolences once again and I followed by saying, "Emily, I know this is a weird scenario, but I just don't see what we have to go on at this point. The police have more resources, better leads, more information. All we have is that Tim was an angry custodian who had nothing to do with Stephen's death."

"Did Chief Ramzorin want you to throw in the towel?" Alyssa asked.

"No, actually he didn't, just made me promise that we would be careful."

"And what about Hannigan?" Emily asked. "Is he going to lock us all up if we continue looking?"

"No, I don't think so."

"Then we should keep looking as long as we can before our parents kill us. Then that'll be a brand new case."

"Oh, look at Emily with the jokes," I said as I offered her a fist bump. She accepted it and then walked off to go to the bathroom. The water started running in the sink just as Ammon burst through the front door like he had been running away from bees.

"Guys, where's Emily?" he asked as soon as the door closed behind him.

Yeah, they definitely like each other.

"She just went to the bathroom, why?" Alyssa asked.

"Well, you won't believe what I found while I was packing up to leave from work," he said.

My hunger for a new lead was just about to be satisfied as Ammon pulled a tablet from the center of his backpack. I didn't smile, but I knew my face lit up with a new hope, as did Alyssa's.

"How the hell did you get that?" I asked.

"Mr. Donahue and I had similar backpacks," Ammon said as he pointed to the insignia on the straps. "He must've thrown it into my backpack instead of his. It's happened in the past with other things, but..."

Ammon handed the tablet over to me and I tried to turn it on. Nothing happened.

"It's dead. But it takes a micro USB like my cell phone, so lemme plug it in," I said as I practically stumbled across the furniture in my excitement to get it power.

"I can't believe the police haven't made a bigger deal out of this," Alyssa said. "I thought maybe they'd ask us if we knew where it was."

"No, that'd be exposing a weakness. They don't want to do that. They want to show they're in control," I said as I fumbled to get the tablet plugged in.

"I'm sorry I didn't find it earlier. I just had no idea," Ammon said.

"Don't be sorry! That's the last thing you should be," I said. "We had just run out of leads so I'm hoping his tablet will show us something useful."

"Glad I could be of some help," Ammon said with a gleaming smile.

I wanted to sit there and watch the tablet charge like a kid waiting up for Santa Claus, but Alyssa pulled me away. When Emily came out of the bathroom and we told her about the tablet, she had a new feeling of hope as well.

I can't imagine leaving my phone or any other electronic behind for someone to prowl through. Not that I had any naked pictures or anything. Not ones of myself, anyway. Let's just say I hope I don't die around anyone in Alyssa's family when no one else has a phone to use.

We sat in the living area and waited as patiently as we could for the tablet to power back on. To break the silence, Ammon turned on his TV and said, "I can't sit here waiting like this. I must have some other commotion."

I was about to say how I agreed when I heard Stephen's tablet jingle back to life and I jumped up off of the couch.

"You're going to hurt yourself, Jack," Alyssa warned.

"You'd all get a laugh out of it," I said, and then I quietly cheered that his tablet didn't have a password.

"And we agreed not to look through his pictures, right?" Emily asked.

"Says you."

"Jack!"

"Okay, we won't."

Once I got to the tablet's home screen, I noticed it wasn't linked to any cell phone company. Just in case of such an event, I had Ammon's Wi-Fi password saved on my phone and used it to establish the link. Once I made the connection, it was time to start wandering. Where should I start? Facebook or emails—since he's over the age of forty.

After looking over all of the apps, I noticed he had some strange Messaging App I had never heard of before. So I decided to start there because, I'll just blame instinct. But what I hit in his messages was quite the gold mine.

"Find anything yet?" Alyssa asked.

"Well, he's definitely not texting his mother constantly, unless you refer to your mom as *Pookie*."

Yes, I said that right. As I dug through the messages, I found that almost all of them were from this contact simply known as Pookie. I knew it was a pet name. Not the most common one, since it sounds so close to *Dookie*, but hey. To each their own, I suppose.

"Sounds like a girlfriend," Emily commented.

"You never refer to me as that to anyone, do you, Jack?" Alyssa asked.

"No, of course not, *Puddin' Pop*."

Alyssa punched my shoulder lightly and I kept reading. Most of the messages made me blush, to say the least. They really had a lust for one another. I knew Stephen didn't have a ring on when I met him, but I wondered who this girl was and why were they so secretive about her real name? Pookie was just about as obvious as saying *my girlfriend*. But what if she wasn't a girlfriend? Not that I thought she was a drug dealer, but…

"Maybe she's a fling," I said. "I don't know why else he wouldn't save her under her real name."

"I've had friends who would swing several dates," Ammon said, "but they just never saved their numbers at all. They'd have one good night with them and that was it."

Wouldn't that be the life? Or the trip of a lifetime to the doctor. Besides, I have Alyssa, so…

Anyway, I decided to click on her empty photo at the side of one of her messages and jump over to her contact information. That's where I found what we needed.

"It's her address. Let me pull it up."

"We can't use his tablet for any internet purposes. Tell it to me and I'll look it up," Alyssa said.

"Good idea—909 North Shades Boulevard," I said.

Alyssa typed the address on her phone and to see what would come up. Emily and Ammon were standing pretty close to one another as I knelt on the ground with the tablet on my short charger. What would be the plan after we found out where this woman was?

"Wow, that's not too far from here, and it's a super nice neighborhood," Alyssa said.

"Okay, so what now?" Emily asked.

"You guys don't expect to just appear on her doorstep to ask questions, do you?" Ammon asked.

Chapter Eight

Saturday Night

I was able to convince Alyssa and Emily that we should at least check Pookie's house out. Ammon, on the other hand, refused to go. The only real perk of bringing Ammon was that we might have been able to cruise in his sleek BMW instead of my poor car. But my car would have to do.

At about eight o'clock, we exited the interstate to make our way down to their house. As Alyssa said, it was a nicer neighborhood. I only worried about the possibility of security cameras all over the property, but hopefully, she didn't have any. Besides, I knew how to spot them before I would run right up to the house.

"What is the plan, Jack?" Alyssa asked.

"Nothing too complicated. We'll park out of sight and see if we can spot anything suspicious."

"So, a stakeout?" Emily asked.

"Basically."

Emily sure knew how to make things more exciting. Well, so did Alyssa, but the mention of our adventure being my first official stakeout got my blood flowing. And the extra blood flow would be helpful for the long wait that was ahead. Hmmm, maybe this wouldn't be as exciting as I thought.

"We'll just make sure we stay out of her immediate sight when we park. Otherwise, she may see us."

"You're the driver, so I'd say that's your responsibility," Alyssa said as she watched the GPS.

"How close are we?" I asked.

"After this stoplight, we're going to turn right into that neighborhood. See the entrance over there with all the trees and shrubbery?"

I leaned over the steering wheel and saw the front entrance. The metal letters spelled out, Whispering Estates.

Wonder what they're all whispering about?

The light turned green and I pulled forward so I could turn right into the neighborhood. My car stuck out like a sore thumb as I saw all the pristine

Mercedes, BMWs, Audis, and so on.

"We really should've taken Ammon's car."

The houses at the entrance all looked like they were built in the late '60s, but they were all definitely redone on the inside. Most of them had large rectangular windows at the front to expose the riches inside. Or, it was for the neighbors to compete with each other on who had the best tree when Christmas time rolled around. Either way, it was surprising how willing everyone was to show off the insides of their homes.

But as we moved farther into the neighborhood, the dwellings became more modern and varied from one another.

"Pookie must have a great job," I said.

"Or, God forbid, Mr. Donahue was sleeping with a married woman," Emily said.

"Did he ever talk about his love life when you worked alongside him? Did anyone ever visit him?"

Emily shook her head.

"He kept everything private. I don't even think he had dude talks with Ammon."

"Hey, just what do you mean by dude talks?"

"Jack, we're pulling up to it."

Alyssa's orders caught my attention and I looked around at the houses. Some of them had fancy fake gold numbers on their mailboxes while others had their numbers painted onto their curbs. When we passed house 913, I knew we were close.

"There."

Alyssa pointed forward at a two-story white house on the corner and I pulled up to the curb on the way to it. In front was a half-moon driveway and on the side was a short driveway leading into a two car garage. Instead of the invasive window being on the front of the house with the half-moon drive, it was on the side that we were facing from my car.

I killed my headlights as I saw two figures in the living room. One was a petite black female sitting down, looking slightly distraught from what I could observe at a distance, the other was a nicely dressed man, also black, walking back and forth talking to her. A gray Mercedes C300 sat out front, ready for a night on the town.

"Well, she's not alone. And hopefully, that's not the killer in there with her," Emily said.

"No, I doubt it. I have a feeling they're married," I said as I went ahead and killed my engine as well.

"So we're just going to wait here?" Alyssa asked.

"Unless some other opportunity arises," I said.

We all went quiet as the man stopped pacing and the woman I assumed was his wife pointed towards the large window we were observing them through. She didn't seem to be pointing at us and I couldn't tell what she was saying, but the man seemed annoyed as he turned around and made his way to the window.

"Do you think they've seen us?" Emily asked.

"This would be a weird reaction if they had."

He bent over and cracked the window open to let in the cool air from outside, then walked back over to her.

"So, Jack…"

I didn't want to waste any time. I jumped out of the car and started sneaking over to the house. This was my chance to hear them talking rather than sit two houses down and guess what they were discussing.

"Jack!" Alyssa whispered harshly as I made my way over.

I shushed them and ran diagonally in the darkness to get to the side of the window, the side closest to the back of the house. No one saw me as I crept up, though I felt like a dirty peeping Tom.

But then, their voices filled my ears and I was ready to try and solve this once and for all.

"… but as I've said, as good as business is, I can't help but think about retirement every day," the man said.

"Retirement? You just turned forty, Derrick."

Okay, the man's name is Derrick. *Got it.*

"Alicia, I plan on retiring when I'm fifty whether you think it's possible or not."

And the woman's name is Alicia. *Great, moving on.*

"And sell the company you created?"

"Let someone else deal with it. I don't want to do it forever. Besides, designing and manufacturing work boots for the future isn't that exciting."

I peeked around and saw Derrick step over to a plush couch that faced the window. He placed his hands on the back of it to release some weight from his legs.

"I'm excited to see Melissa and Jared tonight at The Monte Falco, but I have a feeling they're going to talk about what everyone else is talking about."

"Didn't we just agree not to talk about that?"

"Or him."

Five bucks says they mean Stephen.

"Derrick, please. If they do mention him, don't make it so obvious that you hate him."

"Hate him? That would imply that I hate you too."

"I just," Alicia started. "I didn't think it would be that big a deal based on our agreement."

"Our agreement had boundaries, and you stepped over the boundary that we placed. Alicia, as much as I hate to say this, I feel like I can only truly forgive you now because Stephen's dead."

Now, two sounds decided to happen at the same time: one warranted, the other, not the best timing.

The first, Alicia's gasp when it looked like she might slap him. The second, my freaking cell phone—ringing loud and proud—breaking everyone's concentration into little pieces.

I grabbed at my jeans pocket and cursed to myself as I darted away from the window and found the nearest shrubbery I could hide behind. I heard Derrick march towards the window as I ran off, but I guess he didn't investigate any further. With my heart racing in a 400-meter dash, I yanked out my phone to see who it was.

"Hi. Hello. Yes. Hey Mom, what's going on?" I asked, sounding more frantic than was good.

"Uh, Jack?"

"Sorry, I've been, exercising," I said, trying to catch my breath.

"Okay, well never mind that. Where the hell are you guys?"

"Oh, you didn't get my text?" I asked as I wrapped myself in a lie. "My car battery went out this morning and all the local stores here are out of batteries, so, I have to wait until tomorrow to get one."

"They're out of car batteries? Even the mechanics in town?"

I saw Derrick close the window and I felt a little more comfortable with how loud I could talk.

"Yeah, every single one. It's the damnedest thing."

"Language."

"It's the darnedest thing."

My mom sighed on the other end. I knew she didn't believe me 100%, but when do parents ever? That's just crazy to think that ever happens.

"Jack, please, just tell me if there's something going on. Seriously, anything at all."

I wanted to talk to my mom on the phone, but I started to hear the owner of the shrubbery I was hiding in come out with two stinky bags of trash. So I did what everyone does in a comedic movie, even though it's not convincing whatsoever.

"Mom, I'd—sometimes—signal—cuts out randomly—I can't hear you..."

Hanging up the phone, I stuffed it back into my pocket so there wasn't any light coming from the bushes. When I saw the man glance over, I noticed I was breathing too loudly, so I tried calming down. The man took another second to look around, belched tremendously, and went back into his house.

I sighed, turning back towards the Martin residence as soon as my mind started to calm—just in time to see the Mercedes Benz rip out of the driveway.

Time to head back to my car, but Alyssa was way ahead of me. She pulled up and waved me over. I ran to her, did one last look around, and climbed in.

Chapter Nine

"Jack, what the hell were you thinking?" Alyssa hissed as we pulled away from the curb.

"Do you know where The Monte Falco is?" I asked as I clicked my seat belt in.

"Yeah, probably the most expensive place up this way," Emily chimed in from the back seat.

"Is that where they're going to eat?" Alyssa asked, already sounding as though she was less mad at me.

"That's what they said. Mentioned meeting up with some friends of theirs, Melissa and Jared? Sound familiar? Someone Stephen might've talked about?"

Alyssa and Emily shook their heads. I sighed, picking some newly found leaves on my clothes.

"Did they say anything else?" Alyssa asked.

"Yeah, actually they did," I said, though my memory had already started becoming fuzzy from all the excitement. "The husband, Derrick, said something about an agreement that they had together, and how his wife, Alicia, broke it. And then, he said…"

Alyssa and Emily waited with growing anticipation, but I hated to say it.

"He said, he thinks he could only forgive her because Stephen's dead."

"Jesus!" said Emily, obviously shocked. "Sounds like a guilty man to me."

"I wish I could agree, but I didn't hear them say anything else. My phone rang and I had to run off."

"You left your phone on ring while snooping?" Alyssa asked.

"Yeah, yeah, I know. My bad. Should have had it on vibrate."

"Well, who called you anyway?"

"My mother."

We all actually seemed more nervous about my mother catching on to what was going on than the fact we were chasing a possible killer. The other side of my mind was wondering how we could get into the restaurant, how we could spy on Derrick and his wife. I wasn't sure exactly how spying on them would help. I wasn't even sure I had a full idea or grasp of what was going on. Did Derrick kill Stephen out of revenge? Did Alicia? What was the agreement they had and how was it broken?

"I want to say this is some kind of crime of passion, but, if we could listen to their conversation at the restaurant-"

"I don't think we can. It's reservation only, and expensive as hell," Emily said.

"Well, don't one of you know a guy? Or a gal?" I asked.

"Yeah, I know a guy," Alyssa said with a smile. "Otherwise I wouldn't be driving over to The Monte Falco right now."

First, Alyssa knew the computer geek at the university. Now she knows a guy at a super fancy restaurant?

"Baby, I thought you weren't all that social," I said, referring to the high school Alyssa that I was accustomed to.

"College changes a person, babe," she replied.

"I feel like I don't even know you anymore," I said dramatically, and we all had a laugh.

The laugh helped relieve the tension as we continued on to the restaurant. The night was becoming cool and crisp and I knew summer wasn't here quite yet. The street lights glowed orange onto the plain gray streets, and the stop lights and fancy business signs were the only contrasting colors to the darkness and the orange.

The income level of the area we were driving through seemed to dip and then fly right back up as we drew closer to the restaurant. Alyssa explained how the restaurant was smack dab in the middle of the downtown area. There were all kinds of people out on the streets: young couples trying to go out and make memories that would last a lifetime, and adults wanting to drink enough to forget every mistake they'd ever made.

I took a long look at the restaurants I had never heard of, but I was sure Alyssa and Emily had grown accustomed to in their time out here. It made me think about Mike's Grill and how Stephen had treated us to the meal, only to be found dead just moments later.

Well, that's why we're out here doing this for him.

"Okay, I think we're just about there," Alyssa said.

"Good, I'm kind of hungry," I said.

Alyssa turned right and I saw an oddly shaped sign poking out perpendicular from the older building. Bold white text shouted the restaurant's name, followed by a quiet whisper below that explained it was a Grill and Bar. A few people stood outside like it was a new nightclub, and I saw an Audi pull away from the curb and disappear down the street. That's when I saw the Mercedes Benz pull up. Derrick and Alicia stepped out, handed the key fob to the valet, and walked like royalty past the line into the restaurant.

"I was about to ask where the parking is," I started.

"They move all the cars to an empty lot on the other side of the street," Alyssa said.

"Hope they watch over the cars with tight security," I observed, since it was like watching a *Forbes* 10 Most Expensive Cars list come to life.

As Alyssa began to pull up next to the restaurant, she said, "Hey, I guess Brandon will be our valet."

She did a mildly illegal U-turn to get into position. My car was a piece of shit compared to all the other that had passed through. I mean, it was fourteen years old, but I didn't have the money or the desire for a new one. Besides, it got the job done.

We were met with a few dirty looks from the line outside as we stepped out of the Impala. I could tell we weren't appropriately dressed for the restaurant, either.

Alyssa's scrawny friend Brandon ran on up to us and gave Alyssa a quick hug along with a "Hello." Did it make me jealous? Maybe a little bit. I am known to be territorial. Or is it better to say possessive? Actually, I don't think either one sounds good.

"Do you think Vinh will get us a table?" Alyssa asked.

Brandon ran around to the driver's side of my car and said, "Gosh, I really don't know. We're pretty booked tonight, Alyssa. But go on inside and find out."

Brandon hopped in my car and left us in the dust. We turned away and made our way inside, still getting dirty looks from all the designer dressed individuals outside.

"So you don't know a guy, you know two guys?" I asked.

"Shut up, Jack," Alyssa replied.

Rude.

The restaurant was exquisite and dark in its tone. Waiters wore tight-fitting, spotlessly white button-ups, black slacks that appeared to be dry-cleaned daily, and black bow ties that resembled a perfect demo of how they should be tied. The lighting was dim due to random pieces of black fabric slewing from the ceiling, making outlandish shadows across the floor. And, as fancy as the place was, I couldn't smell a thing. Not a single odor floated around. Everything was either contained in the kitchen or probably in the bathroom.

The front podium had a wall behind it, and the ovular opening to the dining area is how I got my first look at the design. It was cool, to say the least, although if I owned a restaurant, I'd never take the time to do that.

To our luck, Alyssa's suave Asian friend Vinh stood behind the podium.

"Alyssa! Do you finally have that five bucks you owe me?" he asked with a perfect smile. He didn't have an accent and was dressed nicer than all the other waiters. I appreciated Alyssa for not leaving me when she moved out here.

"Vinh, you're always changing your mind on whether or not you want me to pay you back," Alyssa argued.

"Oh, and Emily—almost didn't see you there. And you must be Jack! Yes, I've seen all the photos on Facebook. What a sweet couple."

I would have chatted with him, but we didn't really have the time. Alyssa knew that, too, so she cut to the chase.

"Look, I'll give you five dollars if you can seat us next to that lovely couple that just waltzed in."

"The Martins? Why?"

"It's kind of a long story," Alyssa said. "We just need to sit by them if we can, please?"

Vinh's smile disappeared as he looked down at the seating chart.

"Well, they're in a semi-private room," Vinh said.

I thought all hope was lost, until I figured out he was doing a "bad news/ good news" explanation.

"The table across from them is empty and the family that reserved it is ten minutes late. You could sit there and I'll try to hold off the others if they come in. How long will you need? I can tell you're not going to eat."

He looked us all up and down due to our attire and I said, "We won't need long. We just need to head on over now, please."

"Very well, then."

Vinh stepped from behind the podium and politely asked the couple who just walked in to wait for his return. He walked fast and I could tell he was a regular at some gym nearby. I had to do a light jog to keep up with him, and most of the attendants at the restaurant gave us little to no attention now that they had fresh bread in their faces. When we arrived at the other end of the restaurant, Vinh pointed down the hallway and said, "Third room on your right. That'll get you right next to the Martins."

"Thanks, Vinh," I said, and I handed him a five-dollar bill. "Now leave my girlfriend alone."

Vinh was amused at my comment, but I walked past him without giving him any more attention. It's not that I didn't like the guy, he just reminded me of a certain type that I didn't care to be around. Guys like him, and the families from over the top TV commercials.

Without menus or any guidance from the wait staff, we made our way to the third semi-private dining room on the right. What does semi-private mean? Well, basically, you and your fellow eating companions share a circular room with one side cut out to face the hallway. If I looked at it from a ceiling view, I knew it'd look like a bunch of figure eights stacked on each other with one side missing. It was a strange design, since you could stare into the room across from you without any issues, but also made it perfect for eavesdropping on the Martins and whoever their friends were.

Alyssa and Emily stepped into the dining room first and I turned my head to make sure the Martins were there. They had ordered an appetizer with their friends Melissa and Jared, but the fried delicacy wasn't lifting their spirits much. It was obvious they all had something on their minds, something specific and dark. I had a feeling I knew who they were thinking about.

BAM!

Wanting to jump out of my skin, I banged my knee against the chair that I was supposed to sit in. I cursed softly to myself as Emily and Alyssa turned back towards me. I felt slightly embarrassed, but I mainly didn't want to make a scene that distracted the Martins from their meal.

"Be careful, kid," I heard Derrick say with a light-hearted tone. "But I get it can be nerve-racking to be on a date with two women at once."

Alicia told him to hush up, but I did a friendly wave to them. Alyssa wasn't bothered by his comment, or not visibly, anyway. On the other hand, Emily did blush. But we all sat down and decided to move on from the incident.

A waiter came by promptly.

"What would we like to drink?" the guy in his early twenties asked.

"Water," I said.

"Water," Alyssa said.

"I'll just have water," Emily added.

The waiter looked over the three of us, rolled his eyes, and said, "I figure you guys will be big tippers."

Emily was shocked by his response, but we all shared a laugh. What a fierce dude.

When he left us, I lifted the menu to my face and acted like I was browsing through it. I'm glad I wasn't taking two women on a date to this place. Even taking one would make my wallet shiver.

With my back to them, I heard Alicia saying that she felt bad for me. Lucky for me, none of them knew why I bumped my knee into the chair. They probably thought I was staring at my cell phone like most nineteen-year-olds would. But then, the conversation broke off into something else.

Jared started, "Wow, these fried wontons are really good."

"Didn't we have them the last time we ate here?" Melissa asked.

"No, I think we had the spinach artichoke dip," Jared corrected.

"Oh, yeah."

The four of them fell silent once again. I guessed injuring my knee would be the best part of their meal. The silence was awkward, and I wanted to say they were happily chewing on their appetizer, but as crunchy as the wontons were, I didn't hear any crunching. The tension was running high. Someone had to say something.

"So, we're not supposed to talk about Stephen, or we are?" Jared asked, finally breaking the silence.

Alicia and Melissa seemed ashamed at the mention of his name, and Derrick tried keeping his cool.

"What is there to talk about?" Derrick asked.

"I know you guys were close friends, so I wanted to ask if you heard anything else about the investigation."

"No, I haven't," Derrick said briskly with no other follow up.

I couldn't understand what Melissa was saying under her breath to Jared, but it wasn't good. She was mad at him. He wasn't supposed to mention Stephen. *But why not?*

Alyssa and Emily both gave me a look and I knew they were listening in on the conversation, too. I wished there was a way to discuss their conversation amongst us as we listened, but texting would only distract me from listening. It was proven. Just ask my mom.

A different waiter brought us the waters and left us alone once again. Maybe Vinh had informed them that we weren't there for the outlandishly priced dishes. What a shame.

For some reason, Jared dared to keep talking about Stephen. Maybe he knew Stephen the best out of everyone, or maybe he liked talking about misery.

"The news doesn't seem to know of any family members to speak to. It's sad."

"Delivering the news to those loved ones would be the sad part. Not the fact that others have to be left behind to wallow in pain."

"Derrick, do you want me to change the subject?"

Derrick scoffed and spat, "I think I've made that pretty *fucking* obvious."

A commotion erupted behind us. Emily and Alyssa leaned back in their chairs and I thought Derrick was going to assault Jared. But when I turned around, I saw a different story unfolding.

Hannigan and Flores marched into the semi-private room with their badges out, and Hannigan stated who they were.

"… and we'd like to ask you some questions about Stephen Donahue."

"Yeah, who doesn't?" Derrick asked aloud, irritated beyond belief. "But why?"

"You're the prime suspect in his murder."

The weight of Hannigan's words hit like nothing else. First, because of their heaviness and second, because they didn't feel right. But I didn't have much extra time to react to the accusation. As Hannigan cuffed Derrick and read the rest of the Miranda rights, Flores' eyes stabbed into mine as she demanded, "You need to come with us, too."

I held the stare with her for a second or two, but then reached to the table to grab a piece of paper and followed her out.

Chapter Ten

The crumpled up piece of paper from the restaurant stayed secured in my fist as I rode in the back of Flores' black sedan. Her face scowled as she drove through the night toward the station. I had no idea where it was, but it was outside of the downtown area, that was for sure. Hannigan had put Derrick in a separate car, and Derrick hadn't said a word on the way out of the restaurant. He didn't argue, didn't resist arrest, nothing. Which definitely made me wonder.

I mean, granted, if I were innocent, I might make a scene of some sort as I was taken out; but I feel like guilty people would do the same as well. They showed footage of men and women getting arrested when I was in class this last semester. Most of the arrests were not very smooth. Even if you channel surf past the show *Cops*, you can tell that's the case.

But Derrick, with all of the anger and resentment he'd shown towards Stephen and his passing, appeared to give in. As if he knew this was coming, as if he knew that he would be the one who was brought in for Stephen's murder. And the only reason he'd been prepared was because, well, maybe he did it.

"Okay, Sampson, out of the car."

Flores grabbed my shoulder in an unfriendly way and I stepped out of the vehicle before she had to yank me. Hannigan and Derrick were a ways ahead of us, entering the light of the police station. Flores made sure we weren't right behind them, but once they were in, we followed suit.

Flores was strong, but didn't show it through her finely tailored clothing. She could take care of herself, and I felt like it had been that way for her for most of her life. Hannigan was strong, too, and handled Derrick well. And he wasn't a man I'd mess with. Maybe that's why Hannigan was such a good partner. They definitely didn't have a love interest between them. Not even if the two of them got drunk some night after a long day of questioning assholes.

And now, as the elevator departed with Derrick and Hannigan, I started to wonder why Flores had detained me. Sure, I was at the restaurant spying on the Martins, but I could just say it was a coincidence.

No, lying to the detectives was not my best option. I knew I was in trouble. I knew this wasn't a game; but it never was a game for me.

So I offered, "Aren't you curious as to how we found them?"

The elevator doors opened and we stepped in. Flores leaned over to press the right floor and then she spoke to me.

"Not really. We pulled his phone records, which is what led us to believe Derrick may have done it."

"What evidence do you have?" I asked.

The elevator doors opened and she led me down a narrow hallway with doors on all sides. They were interrogation rooms, only about four of them available.

"None-yuh."

I was surprised at the response Flores gave me. But she didn't seem to find humor in it. She kept a straight face as she pointed to a blank gray room on one side of the hallway and said, "Just go on in there and have a seat."

As we stepped up to the door, I fake-stubbed my toe on the threshold, but only to distract her from the paper I pressed into the strike.

"Jesus, if you finish out college to be a detective, you'll be a clumsy one."

She pulled me away from the threshold and redirected me forward into the room. I quickly took a seat and watched as she closed the door to make sure my trick had worked.

She closed it slowly and I bit my lip, anticipating the clicking of the door closing. I knew the click wouldn't happen, but I worried that Flores would notice the lack of sound. And just as the door closed, someone called her and she left the door how it was.

If it was anything like the interrogation rooms we were allowed to view on the fall field trip, the doors only lock on the inside, hence the reason I shoved the paper into the door. I never heard the click, so I stood up and tried to listen out in the hallway. When I heard no footsteps, I pulled on the door and found that my little trick had worked. Success!

I quietly stepped into the hallway and looked left, right, and then left again—like the corridor was a busy intersection. I didn't see any movement or hear any noises, so I figured that Derrick was in the only other closed room. I crept over to the door, pushed it open, and stepped on in.

Derrick's head came up as the door closed, but the sight of me immediately puzzled him. He was distraught; his eyes were red, and I could hear his breathing across the room.

"Who are you?" he asked.

"A junior detective," I said as I sat across from him.

"Really? That's funny."

"Glad you find humor in it."

He looked me over a few more times, and he knew I was lying. Of course I was lying. I would not want to work under Flores.

"I'm really here because, well, truth be told, I don't think you killed Stephen. But they think you might have, for whatever reason."

"So I'm supposed to trust you, and tell you everything? How old are you, twenty-two?"

"No, nineteen, but thanks," I said.

Derrick grunted and I knew it would take a little more to get him to talk. After all, I wasn't really a junior detective.

"I'm in here because I may be the only friend you have. And Stephen was a friend of mine, and you seem to be a friend of his."

"What does that make us? Friends of mutual friends?"

"It doesn't matter," I said firmly. "Tell me what's going on. I know you didn't do this."

"I had every reason to, though," Derrick said as his head fell and he stared at the table in despair.

"Derrick, you gotta tell me what happened," I pleaded.

"The dean, Stephen, he was a good friend of mine. He was kind. He always wanted to help people, didn't have an attitude or cause any problems…"

I wondered why Derrick wasn't saving this speech for the funeral, until he spoke the final sentence.

"But, he was a ladies man."

That's when I thought about the conversation with his wife that I had spied on, and how he reacted at the restaurant. I had a feeling I knew what his reasoning would have been, but he explained it to me, anyway.

"My wife slept with Stephen a few weeks ago. Well, I'm sure it's been more times than that. But she admitted it to me a few weeks ago. I would have been fine with it if it had been anyone else, but…"

"Why would you have been okay with it?" I asked.

"Alicia and I are in an open relationship. We're not completely monogamous. It's an agreement we made at the beginning of it all. Even back when we were dating, we knew it was weird for some people to hear; I know that. It's weird for me to talk about it."

"So she *spent the night* with Stephen even though he was off limits?"

Derrick nodded.

"I made the mistake first—at the beginning of our relationship—back in college. She had a friend, Cheryl, I think that was her name. They were best friends at the time. And one night, we almost made it together, but, we were rudely interrupted."

He sighed and I could tell he was blushing.

"Anyway, from then on we decided to search for couples who would want to exchange partners. Went to bars for swingers, and then the internet came around and that made things easier. But we agreed on couples only. No best friends, no random singles. Just couples we could trade with."

"And you would've killed Stephen over it?"

"I was mad...but I didn't want to kill anyone. And I never have."

"Would you have hired someone else to kill him?"

Derrick looked at me with a pained face and said, "No, I wouldn't do that, either."

I wasn't really sure if there was anything else I could ask him. Nothing was really coming to mind. The main reason was that I believed him. I believed everything he said. I didn't understand it at all, especially the open relationship part. Still, I believed him.

But before I could say anything else, the door swung open behind me and I turned around. Hannigan and Flores stood there in the doorway, obviously displeased.

"Oh, I just thought you'd want to interview us both," I said.

Chapter Eleven

Sunday, around 2 a.m.

Flores practically threw me out of the interrogation room and had me sit in the original room alone; which, by the way, did not have a cell phone signal whatsoever. So I was stuck there by myself, mulling over the details in my mind.

They questioned Derrick for hours. I didn't know if they were getting more information out of him than I gave them or if they dragged it out just to make me suffer. I couldn't hear a word of what they were saying, and this time, I was really locked into the room. No paper tricks.

But as I felt it growing later in the night, I stood up and pranced around the space, trying to find a signal. When I finally did, the text messages flooded in.

They were from Alyssa, Emily, and probably Ammon, since I didn't recognize the number. I didn't read through all the messages. They mostly said the same thing: "Where the hell are you?"

I sent a simple reply, asking them to come get me from the station. I tried remembering the cross streets and sent them that information, along with an apology. The text took a while to finally send, and I wondered when Flores would storm in and execute me.

It wasn't too long.

She stepped in and closed the door behind her. I was standing up against the wall on the other side of the room and she didn't like that.

"Sit down, Jack."

Flores wasn't in the mood for me to joke around. I wasn't in the mood either, after being stuck in a blank gray room for several hours.

I sat down and she remained standing. She placed both palms on the table and leaned in towards me. Not for a kiss or anything affectionate. But rather...

"Now I want you to listen to what I'm about to say, and I want you to listen good. Did you clean your ears this morning? Do I need to get a Q-tip first?"

I shook my head.

"You're smart, Jack. I'll give you that. You have determination. The unprofessional side of me wants to admire you. However, I'm on the clock, and I don't like the idea of finding you and your friends dead because you're running around trying to solve this case, a case that Hannigan and I are on, one that we can take care of ourselves. Our *job* is to solve this case. Your job is to run on home to your friends and family and have a good rest of the summer while you're still young. Whatever relationship you had with Stephen, it's not going to help your investigation. It's only going to cloud your judgment. Happened to a detective friend of mine in California when her husband, well, he wasn't the man she thought he was."

"Seems to happen a lot, nowadays," I said.

Flores returned a distant stare before she nodded and finished, "I'm going to let you go. But I hope this warning resonates with you."

Flores started towards me to lead me from my chair, but I asked, "Is this a final warning, or second to final?"

She turned to me and smiled, but it wasn't a friendly smile. More of a "just try me" kind of smile.

I stood up from my chair and followed her outside.

"Need a ride?" she asked.

"No, I think those pesky friends of mine are going to pick me up," I replied, thinking I'd better send a text now that my phone had signal.

"Good."

Flores took out her pack of cigarettes and made sure she was downwind of me. The toxins did a slow sway in the night and I heard a few crickets singing their song of loneliness. I felt half dead. It was weird to think that just a day ago, I was driving out to get Alyssa and Emily so we could run away back to Stanton. Now I felt stuck here until I could figure out what was going on.

The familiar BMW pulled off the street and into the driveway of the station. I wasn't insulted that they brought Ammon's car instead of mine, even though I'm mentioning it now.

They pulled up next to me and I stepped towards the back seat. Once I was inside, Alyssa hugged me like we hadn't seen each other in years. I embraced it, and it helped wake me up a bit.

"You okay, babe? They didn't beat you around or anything, did they?" she asked, kissing my rugged face with her soft lips.

I felt a shiver down my spine and smiled.

"No, that's just for you to do."

Alyssa pushed me away and I heard Ammon chuckle in the front seat.

Being with my group again made me feel a little more rejuvenated, but I knew that Ammon's couch would be cushioning my body in a matter of minutes, which didn't really help keep me awake.

"Ready to talk?" Alyssa asked. "Why did they keep you so long?"

"Well, I wasn't the most cooperative detainee."

"What did you do?" Emily asked.

"I snuck into Derrick's interrogation room."

"Derrick Martin?" Ammon asked.

"Yeah?" I replied dumbly.

"He and Stephen were such good friends, though. And they think he did it?"

I nodded and added, "But Derrick denies it, even though he didn't put up much of a fight when he was detained."

"Derrick's a peaceful man. Came by the school all the time," Ammon said.

"Yeah, well, the police are pretty sure it was him. And they have a motive."

"What's the motive?" Emily asked.

"Derrick and Alicia are in an open relationship, but they did have a few boundaries, one of which Alicia crossed."

"Stephen had sex with Alicia?"

"Yeah, Derrick said that Stephen was quite the ladies' man, and even after he specifically requested that they not do anything together."

The news disappointed Emily and Ammon, and even Alyssa. They all looked up to Stephen; thought he couldn't find the right woman when, in reality, he just couldn't get enough of them. Not that having sex with people is a bad thing. But maybe he should have narrowed his sights on the wife of someone else— someone who'd be okay with it. Or even better, a single woman.

"That could drive a man over the edge," Ammon said.

"It could, and has before, but I don't buy it. I don't think Derrick would do something like that," Emily argued.

"Me neither," Alyssa said.

I took in their thoughts and nodded my head.

"Yeah, I don't think he did it. There was something about the way he was talking to me in the interrogation room, besides how he denied doing it."

"Well, if Derrick didn't do it, then who did?" Ammon asked.

"Do you have his tablet? Maybe we can find more on it," I suggested.

"I think Emily grabbed it before we left the apartment," Ammon said as he looked to Emily.

She had her purse at the ready and slipped the tablet out of it.

"Something I'm sure you didn't think about, Jack, but I have it ready to hook up to the hotspot connection on my phone, or else it's useless," Emily said.

"Well, look at you," I said. But as I pressed on the screen, I noticed it wasn't responding. "Is it dead?"

"No, we just turned it off. Someone kept calling through some app," Emily explained.

I made a face at Emily, showing that I was disappointed that she didn't answer. She shrugged, and Ammon caught onto our silent argument.

"I told her never to answer a dead man's phone...er, tablet, in this case," he explained.

Strange advice. Or maybe I'm just nosy.

The tablet came back to life like the hero of an action movie who we knew wasn't dead all along, and the notifications started buzzing in from an app called Phone Away From Phone. The vamp's voice from Sesame Street came to mind.

One missed call... two missed calls... three missed calls... four missed calls, ah, ah, ah!

But once those notifications stopped buzzing, a new one popped up saying that there was a new voicemail as well.

I pressed the notification for the missed calls and saw all four were from the same person. A contact named Lois. Looking through his call log, she appeared to contact him about once or twice a week, and sometimes more.

"Well, this is definitely a better name than Pookie. Any of you know someone named Lois?" I asked.

Everyone shook their heads.

"Well, let's meet her."

I pressed the notification for the voicemail.

"You have one new message," the automated voice said. "First new message."

The recording began with Lois on the other end of the line. The mood was set instantly when the silence was only filled with sniffles and soft breathing. I didn't think she would talk, that she might just hang up the phone and give up. She knew he was dead. Her voice was troubled, soft, and hurt.

"I just..." Lois started on the recording. "I just wanted to hear your voice again, that's all."

I glanced up and saw Emily, half turned in the front seat, staring at the tablet in my hands. Even in the dim light, I could see her look of devastation.

Lois waited a few more seconds on the other line and then ended the call. Emily fell farther into sadness as Alyssa and I shared a look of grief. The message wasn't easy to listen to, and I had no intention of replaying it. Ammon attempted to console Emily as he continued his drive towards the apartment. I checked further into the contact information for Lois and found her address. When I pressed on it, the GPS came up and showed her house wasn't too far from the university.

I wondered if it would be a good idea to pay her a visit in the morning— alone. The idea swam around in my mind as I curiously backed out of her information and checked more of Steven's contacts.

"I bet he has more addresses in here than the county registry," I said in disbelief.

"So, what's next, Jack?" Alyssa asked.

I sighed, not knowing exactly what to say. It seemed like a good idea to go to Lois' place in the morning, but I had a feeling they wouldn't want to hear it.

"How about we just get back to the apartment and get some sleep. It's been a long day."

Chapter Twelve

Late Sunday Morning

I know I told everyone that I was ready to go to bed that night before we got back to the apartment, but my young detective mind kept rolling non-stop, thinking about everyone involved in the case so far.

A random robbery gone wrong? No, definitely not. Someone killed Stephen for a reason. Plus, he wasn't robbed. Not to my knowledge, anyway.

The janitor: again, definitely didn't kill him. Had a weird alibi, but a believable one. One that could be proven.

Derrick Martin: the police's prime suspect. Why? Because his wife had sex with Stephen, prompting a pretty direct motive. A crime of passion, and anger, and all that stuff you see in the soap operas.

A killer hired by Derrick Martin: It was a thought, but I had a feeling that person didn't exist. If Derrick wanted Stephen dead, he would've done it himself. Especially in a scenario like this.

I held Alyssa from behind as we lay in the living room, but I wasn't falling asleep. My eyes would close, only to open again at a new thought rushing through my brain. It was like a new train was running through every few minutes, making me question everything I had seen so far.

What was bothering me so much? *The video surveillance? The lack of other witnesses? The timing of this murder?*

I'm a believer that everything happens for a reason. So why else would Stephen be killed right when I arrived, if I wasn't supposed to solve the case?

Okay, I'm not that conceited. But I knew Derrick didn't do it, and I had a strong feeling backing that, saying he wasn't involved at all, either. Maybe it was one of the several women on his phone who got too attached and didn't want him sleeping around, but then when he did, *bang*.

A part of me felt as though I was taking too much time on this. I wasn't doing anything to add to the investigation. Maybe I was just sour on the idea of being wrong. Or that the police were capable of solving it before me. But why was I angry about it? We were on the same side. We both wanted to bring Stephen's name justice, and his family, if he had any left. Maybe it bothered me because I knew Derrick didn't do it and that he wasn't involved. But yet, the police had him in questioning as a prime suspect.

Even though I woke up feeling like I didn't get any sleep, I knew I had slept some. But when I saw the clock said 10 a.m., I cursed at myself for not being able to sleep later. So as I had originally planned, I started getting ready and prepared myself for a visit to Lois.

I found my keys among Alyssa's stuff and made my way down to the parking garage. I checked around one more time for creepy lurkers before I climbed into my car. Locking the doors and starting it up, I buckled my seatbelt and took out my cell phone. I typed in the address and pressed Go.

"You're on the fastest route and should reach your location by 10:24 a.m," my GPS informed me.

"How am I on the fastest route if I haven't even moved yet?" I asked as I shifted the car into drive.

The cruise on over to Lois' house was peaceful. I missed having Alyssa and Emily along with me. They seemed to help my thinking process and help me validate or shoot down any ideas I might have. But, alone time is always nice too, in small quantities, and I'm sure they'd be happy to not have me around for a few moments.

Plus, a bunch of annoying teenagers storming up to the house of a grieving woman sounded like a situation where she wouldn't open the door. I had reasoned in my mind that one annoying teenager would be plenty.

Her neighborhood was a less expensive version of the Martins' but with about the same style, and it appeared to be a nice area at first glance. None of the houses showed signs of any recent break-ins; bullet shells didn't litter the streets. Honestly, the neighborhood reminded me of mine back home in Stanton, where we were supposed to be by now.

Well, Mom hasn't assigned a hitman on me yet, or extradition by a US Marshall.

The two-car garage door was down and the square driveway was empty and clean. A few lights were on inside the brick house, but they were very dim. I wondered if she was a churchgoer, being that it was Sunday.

I pulled up in front of her house and put my car in park. I stepped out and made sure my door was locked, mainly because it's a habit, not because I thought the neighbor kids would take my change from the door.

I wasn't very nervous until I started thinking about the whole situation. This visit was very… unprecedented. I'm a kid. Well, legally an adult, but whatever. She might shoo me away, she might explode on me. Who knew. It made me think about when I visited the Millers as I was looking into Sam's suicide. That was easy, though. They didn't think anything of it when I came to talk to them. Well, Mr. Miller eventually did when he gave me a piece of his mind.

Nervousness showered over me as I stepped up to the front door and heard the faint sound of a TV on in the background. Someone was home, or they'd left it on. I was about to find out for sure.

The doorbell played a glittery tune to inform whoever was in the house that someone was there to see them. I heard a smaller sized dog bark; and a woman's voice lightly scolded the dog. I tried peeking through the glass, but it was about as clear as a kaleidoscope—without all the colors. The dog beat her to the door, of course, and then she came along.

"Who are you?" she asked as she tried to peer through the other side.

"I'm not a Jehovah or a salesman."

"That still doesn't make me want to open my door."

I hoped the levity might help, but when it didn't, I said, "I'm a friend of Stephen's."

The woman on the other side of the door fell silent and I waited patiently. Her unclear figure moved and I knew she was going to unfasten the lock. I felt successful in my efforts, until I saw just how devastated she was.

Her eyes were puffed and red from the buckets of tears that had escaped from her. She was tall, but not as skinny as her voice made her sound. Her long, faded blond hair appeared greasy as it was pushed behind her. She wore plain gray sweatpants and a loose-fitting dark T-shirt. A thin brown blanket wrapped her shoulders and she brought over a corner to scratch her small nose for only a moment's time.

It was an acceptable way to dress on a Sunday when you have nowhere to go, but I was surprised she opened the door and revealed herself to me.

She asked, "What's your name?"

"Jack Sampson. Stephen was a family friend of mine. And you're Lois?"

Guilt fell over me as she nodded and said, "Well, Jack, come on in. I wasn't expecting guests, so the house is a mess, but I'd like to talk to you."

Her instant trust in me at the mention of Stephen's name made me hope that no one would take advantage of it. But as she opened the door further, her blond Shih Tzu ran out and started jumping on my leg. The dog panted and smiled gleefully as I leaned over and petted him.

"Buster, stop that," Lois urged.

"That's okay. I like dogs."

I continued petting Buster and Lois smiled. When I looked up, she said,

"He's acting like he did around Stephen. Usually he just keeps barking non-stop."

Buster eventually stepped away from me and Lois called him inside. When I stepped in, she said, "And can you lock the deadbolt?"

I nodded and turned the pseudo-bronze knob to one side till I heard the door lock.

Her house was mainly just one big hallway with the separate rooms sculpted to their own liking. I could tell there was a study on the right, a kitchen to the left, and straight ahead was the living room where the TV was on. She had sliding glass doors to look out in her backyard and to gaze at the swimming pool that had its own white picket fence around it. Her lawn was cut down and bright green, as if someone had recently done a fertilizer commercial. As I walked to the other end of the house, I concluded that it fit my mom's definition of "messy"—a few dishes lingered in the sink with condiment stains; a few books were pulled from the shelf in the study and opened randomly over the desk. The only part of the house that appeared somewhat messy (by my definition) was the living room, where I could tell she had been hanging out constantly since the news broke of Stephen's death. Maybe this woman wasn't just another swing or fling.

She sat down on the couch that faced the TV and turned it off. It was some show like *Meet the Press* or something, so I was happy she turned it off. Then she gestured towards an armchair and said, "You can sit there, if you'd like. Or on the couch. Both are comfy."

I figured the armchair was the best spot to sit and parked myself there. I noticed in the study, and now in the living room, she had an abundance of different items and knick-knacks along with paintings, mainly with Native American undertones. It was different from what I was used to seeing in most homes.

"Do you like history?" I started off.

"I guess I have to, since I'm a historian."

"Ah, well that makes sense."

"I grew up watching *Bonanza* and *Gunsmoke*, and sometimes *Rawhide*. The great American west started to interest me more and more as I grew up. And now, here I am. My next line of college visits will be sometime in September. But in a month or so, I'll be hitting the road for some conferences in Kansas and Oklahoma."

I nodded as Buster jumped up on my lap and begged for my attention. I didn't make him wait very long.

Lois produced a sad smile as I scratched his tummy and then she said, "You can probably tell I wasn't the kid everyone wanted to play with in school."

"They wanted to play cops and robbers; you wanted to play cowboys and Indians."

She nodded.

"Those damn brothers of mine."

I felt that we were both still analyzing each other. She wanted to make sure I was trustworthy, and I wanted to make sure her dog wouldn't pee on me sporadically. That's what happened with the last Shih Tzu I was in contact with.

Her eyes darkened as she focused in on the elephant in the room.

"So, you knew Stephen? Or, your family knew Stephen?"

"Yes, he was a friend of my father's."

"I knew the name Sampson sounded familiar. I think I remember Stephen saying he was going to a funeral a few years back for…"

Lois hadn't been thinking, but her words only stung me for a second.

"It was your father, right? I'm so sorry."

I didn't hate talking about my father's death. He was a soldier. Of course there was a possibility he'd get killed. We just never thought it would happen.

Now, with my heart racing and my mind out of focus—and the everlasting flurry of thoughts and memories of me and my father being together—I said, "Uh… no, it's okay. It feels like forever ago."

Lois sympathized as she said, "That's how I feel about Stephen, already. I feel like it's been years. But it was only Friday, was it?"

"Yeah," I said, thinking back on it. Then something mentally slapped me and I knew I had to get back on track. "So, what was your relationship to Stephen?"

Scrunching up her face, she replied, "Did he not talk about me?"

It was then that I wondered, *What's the best way to tell her that we have Stephen's tablet and heard her message and then I investigated?*

"Don't worry, I wouldn't be surprised if he didn't. We were very, on and off."

"My girlfriend and her friend were closer to him than I was, since he lived over here. He would only come to town, mainly when my father was alive. After he was killed overseas, Stephen didn't come over as much."

"Oh, I see," she said, becoming more and more suspicious. "So, why are you here? Or how did you even know to find me? I mean, it's weird that you arrived on my doorstep today, and just last night…"

That's when her eyes widened and I lifted my hands from petting Buster.

"We have his tablet. His assistant ended up with it somehow."

"Ammon did?"

"Yes."

"So you and Ammon listened to my message!"

"Actually, the four of us did, but…"

"Jack!"

Buster looked up from his dazed state of mind and gave us both a "Hey, I'm trying to relax" look. I scratched his head.

"Look, Lois, I'm sorry."

"That's so embarrassing."

"I wouldn't have done it but I feel like they have the wrong man as a prime suspect."

She stayed befuddled with her red face and embarrassed demeanor, but then she appeared normal as she asked, "Who do they have?"

Thinking I might be able to bring her back in, I replied, "Derrick Martin."

Buster's tail softly hitting my leg was the only sound for a few seconds. Lois' eyes diverted to the ground as I saw her mouth Derrick's name. All of the air escaped from her body and she let her head fall into her palms.

"No. No, no, no, there's no way. None of this makes any sense."

"That's why I'm here, Lois. I'm trying to make it all make sense."

"I feel like you're just snooping. That you and your friends are bored and trying to have a fun summer!"

Her comment didn't rub me the right way at all.

"I'm pretty sure we could be doing a lot of other things besides trying to solve a murder. Besides, this isn't my first rodeo."

"You've solved other murders?" she asked, incredulously.

"It's a long story."

Her loud scoff filled the room and Buster's head came up from my lap. I decided I needed to take control of this situation and make it fast.

"Look, Stephen was a friend of mine, and he obviously meant a lot to you. That's why I'm doing this. Ever since his murder, I've felt that there's something more going on. Something more to the idea of someone killing him. I don't think it's a crime of passion on Derrick's part because of Stephen and Alicia's fling or whatever it was, but I can't come to a good explanation as to why he was killed, or who would do it? Stephen was such a good guy: loving, caring, compassionate. He wouldn't cause any harm to anyone. So,

I'm trying to figure out why someone would do this to him. This visit is not to embarrass you or insult you in any way, but rather, to figure out who killed our mutual friend and why. Because based on your reaction, and based on Derrick's reaction, he's innocent. This was someone else, and I need you to help me find this person. If you have any information, any at all that might find Derrick innocent and the right person guilty, speak now, or… I'm sure you know the rest."

Lois heard me just fine but she was still taking everything in and trying to formulate her response. My impromptu speech had caught her off guard, which was exactly what I wanted. I was tired of beating around the bush; I was tired of people questioning my quest for the truth. No one believed it was Derrick except for the police, and that was a problem.

But then, her response was ready.

"Jack, I know you're older than a kid, but in my eyes, you're a kid. And I've always found it funny how kids look at adults in a different light—or when someone dies, we think that Stephen was a flawless man, who wouldn't hurt anyone. Now I agree I don't think Stephen would hurt someone physically. But mentally, emotionally, unintentionally, sure—because he'd done it before. I'm living proof of that. I didn't want to be one of Stephen's flings. I wanted him to be my husband. But he… Ugh, it's not important to say exactly what he did, but I just want you to know, even though you've probably heard it your whole life: no one is perfect.

"As you get older, you'll realize everyone makes mistakes, no matter what size or shape they take on in society. There's no reason to idolize Stephen. I'm glad he was so nice to you and your family, but take those good things and make sure to hold on to them. And as for what I'm telling you, make sure you don't fall into making his same mistakes or the mistakes of others around you. Try to form yourself into a perfect person. Maybe not for everyone, but at least for yourself."

When she was done with her speech, she took a drink from her mug of cold coffee and said in a new tone, "I remember Stephen saying something about being harassed, but he never said who was doing it or why. I asked if he was in any real danger and how long it had been going on."

"When did he tell you all of that?" I asked.

"It was before the beginning of this school year. Like I said, never mentioned a name or what it was about or anything like that."

"Sounds like a vague conversation."

Lois smiled and commented, "As I said, you and I know two different

75

Stephens. A conversation like that was normal between us, sadly."

We stared at each other for a few moments and Buster made a groaning sound. I knew my welcome had been overstayed.

"Well, thank you, Lois. And if you need to call his tablet again, we won't answer or listen to the message," I promised.

"I'd appreciate that," she said softly. "But here's my card if you need anything else."

She had a new shipment of business cards at the ready on her coffee table. I accepted one, and a few moments later, I was back outside on her front porch with Buster pawing at the window for me to come back.

Chapter Thirteen

Later Sunday Afternoon

When I arrived back at the apartment, my actions weren't really questioned. I'd never gotten around to telling Emily, Alyssa, and Ammon where I was going or what was next, but they didn't seem mad that I hadn't. Alyssa only acted hurt that I hadn't wakened her up and made her breakfast, but I played along and said I'd really had to get going.

I told them all about my conversation with Lois, without elaborating too much on the last part and about not knowing the same Stephen. I felt Emily, and possibly Ammon, would be offended by that. I understood what Lois meant, but that still didn't paint a clear picture as to why someone would kill or want to kill Stephen.

"Somebody was harassing him before the school year started?" Alyssa asked.

"That's what Lois told me," I replied, trying to avoid saying, "That's what she said."

"Did he ever say anything like that to you, Ammon?" Emily asked.

Ammon, who'd been ordering pizza, put his cell phone away and replied, "About getting harassed? No. We didn't really talk to each other on that level. But if he was harassed at the beginning of the school year, I wonder how it carried over all the way to now."

I shook my head and Alyssa lightly scratched my back. She knew I was tired.

"I think we're all tired," Alyssa announced.

"Not to mention, my mom sent me plenty of colorful texts that I had the pleasure of reading before you came back," Emily said to me.

"Oh shit, my grandparents are probably flipping out, too," Alyssa said as she checked her phone.

"I think my mom will be able to hold for a little longer. I'm sure she knows the real reason I'm out here by now."

"We get it, Jack, your mom is the coolest."

I laughed at Alyssa's comment and plopped down on the couch. The crisp and cold brown leather contoured to my body as I took a deep breath. My mind had been racing for too long, and now the ridiculous anticipation of the pizza was starting to occupy it.

"What kinds did you get, Ammon?" I asked.

"Well, I can't eat pork, so I got hamburger pizza for me and a cheese and a pepperoni for you three," he responded.

"Oh, okay," I replied. "And you don't have to work today?"

"No, but they may need me tomorrow."

"Gotcha."

Ammon smiled and disappeared into the bathroom. Alyssa and Emily were talking quietly amongst themselves, until Emily got a phone call. So, Alyssa trotted over to the TV in front of me and said, "Well, we could play some Mario Kart?"

She grabbed two sets of Wii controllers and I cried, "You mean we've had Mario Kart this whole time!"

Alyssa turned on the game system and sat down next to me. She bumped her shoulder into me softly and I asked, "What was that for?"

"You'll be getting plenty of it when we start playing here pretty soon," she said with a wink.

"Haha, okay!"

*****

As exciting as Mario Kart first sounded, I realized after the first game that I was already tired of it. Emily had joined us sometime during the first race. About halfway through the second race, I jokingly tossed my controller and Emily gladly picked it up. The plus side was, the pizza guy wasn't too slammed and was able to deliver our food in under thirty minutes, as promised. Which was a good thing, since I already had too many mysteries to solve.

Ammon answered the door and paid for the delivery without ever asking us for any money. He seemed like a nice guy. I just hoped he didn't take advantage of Emily in any way, especially in her current emotional state.

Alyssa and Emily were nearing the end of the third race when Ammon walked the pizzas to the kitchen. That's when my mom's voice nagged me and said I should offer to pay, but as soon as I did, he said, "No, you're guests in my home. I wouldn't have extended this hospitality if I wasn't ready to completely take care of you."

"Completely take care of us? Well in that case, can we all get a massage?"

I joked.

"Not from me," Ammon said with a sneer.

He placed the pizzas on the dining table and made another announcement about their existence. Alyssa and Emily were about to rip each other's heads off as they neared the end of their race, and when Emily won, they both hopped up off of the couch and cheered. Well, Emily cheered. Alyssa jeered.

"That was cheating! I don't know how you just randomly had extra turtle shells."

"Yeah, well, just know I'm the best and you better deal with it!" Emily said as she tried to high five Ammon.

I turned away to face the saddened Alyssa as she said, "I was literally right there."

She used her hands to show how far she was from the finish line, and I grabbed her hands and morphed us into a hug. She kept laughing in my ear and I smiled as I held her back, hoping that nothing would ever take her away from me again.

When we parted, I saw Ammon finishing a conservative kiss on Emily's lips. Ammon then turned away and made sure to grab plenty of paper plates and napkins.

"I'll probably need to get a knife too before you dig into the pizza. Sometimes, they're not the best at cutting them."

I took the plates and napkins from Ammon as he dug around in a drawer he had specified for plastic ware. Alyssa smiled at me as I passed her a plate. Emily was coming down from a blushing spree. Once Ammon threw the plastic knife over to us, we ripped the pizzas apart and I served myself four slices before retreating to the living room yet again.

"What about ladies first?" Alyssa asked.

"Oh yeah, sorry," I said, as I went ahead and took the first bite.

If I had just finished running a mile or two in gym class, I wouldn't have felt like eating for hours. However, having my brain work overtime made me hungrier than anything else.

Alyssa, Emily, and Ammon eventually joined me. The ladies had sprinkled a light amount of Parmesan cheese on their slices, while Ammon had practically covered his in crushed red peppers. I kicked myself for not getting any Parmesan, but Alyssa said that's what I got for rushing.

We sat around, eating pizza and all. Emily offered to get everyone drinks and Ammon went to help her. I stayed on the couch with Alyssa and tried to steal some of her Parmesan. She wasn't very appreciative of that.

"Do you know what Emily's phone call was about?" I asked.

"I think it was her parents. Not sure how the conversation went, I'm afraid."

"They're not freaking out, yet," Emily said from the kitchen as she overheard us. I felt bad for not asking her directly, but Alyssa was right there with me. And I didn't feel like yelling across the apartment.

"Not that I'm trying to kick you guys out, but when do you think you'll head back?" Ammon asked, and I saw him grab Emily's shoulder and rub it affectionately.

"I...I really don't know. I'd like to get to the bottom of this first, but the cops are quite convinced that the killer is Derrick Martin—even though Lois and probably Derrick's wife don't believe that."

"We'll stay as long as we need to, or until you kick us out," Alyssa said.

I appreciated her support, as always. And the way she said it made my whole body tingle, to say the least.

"I thought about just going on home, so your parents don't get upset," I said. "But I just know something else is going on here, especially after my meeting with Lois."

I continued devouring my pizza and they did the same. Why did I have this overwhelming feeling that there's more to this case? I didn't even have any proof of it. Is there really a gut feeling that detectives can develop? Or was I just eating too fast?

I finished my slices of pizza and felt that I could stomach one or two more. I stood up from the couch cautiously and asked if anyone wanted anything else.

"I'll take another breadstick," Ammon said.

"We got breadsticks?" I asked as I headed over.

"Of course. And some ranch and marinara."

"Can't go wrong with that."

As I finished my sentence, I saw Stephen's tablet over on the counter and the screen came to life for a second before falling to black again. I wondered if Lois was calling to hear Stephen's voice, but the screen would've stayed alive longer if she were.

As much as I hated to mess around with a dead man's electronics, my curiosity was getting the best of me. Why would he have a notification? And what did it say?

I stepped over to his tablet and unlocked the screen. The message popped up, but it was a message from the tablet's operating system.

"Are you sure you don't want to have notifications turned on for Kik? You have 9 pending message(s)."

Stephen has a Kik? So he keeps up with multiple women and multiple messaging apps?

Not to sound mean or anything, but some applications were aimed more towards kids and young adults, i.e., Kik. It was a messaging app with cute emojis and such to send. I feel annoying just explaining it.

Anyway, it wasn't an app that I felt like Stephen would use, or anyone above the age of twenty-five or so. Plus, with nine messages pending, someone was obviously trying to get ahold of him.

Pressing the notification threw me into his settings, where I went ahead and turned on any further notifications for Kik. Then, I opened the app and started looking over the messages.

Eight of them were random spam messengers that had their accounts deleted already, but the final one had a weird garbled up name filled with random alphanumerics. The preview of the message said, "Are we still me..."

My nerves went all over the place as I opened the message and read it as loud as I could in my head, over and over.

"Are we still meeting tonight? Let me know if we can still meet at the same spot we discussed before."

I tried scrolling up in the messages but they had all been deleted. This was a brand new message, probably one sent from a different number or account every time. I also felt like it wasn't just some woman or some new fling.

"Jack, how long does it take to get a breadstick?" Ammon called from the living room.

"Just long enough," I said as I grabbed a few breadsticks with dipping sauce and made my way back.

They noticed I had the dean's phone and I could hear their silent groans through their rolling eyes.

"No, no, this is good, trust me."

I handed Ammon his breadstick and sat down. When they saw I wasn't eating and I was fixated on the tablet, they were surprised. I mean, even though we're all addicted to cell phones nowadays.

"What is it, Jack?" Alyssa asked.

"A new lead."

"Like what?" Emily asked.

"Just look."

I placed the phone on the table and everyone took a turn looking at it. Ammon was the last one. He glanced at me and said, "You know what I said about messing with a dead man's phone."

"Yeah, but this time, they don't know he's dead."

"If it's not the person who killed him, then who would it be?" Alyssa asked.

"Only one way to find out."

I started to text a message back, but they stopped me.

"Jack, this can't be a good idea," Emily said.

Ammon nodded and Alyssa seemed concerned.

"What the hell else am I supposed to do?"

"Call the police? Tell them about it?" Alyssa suggested.

"They'll roll up with twenty squad cars and scare this person away."

They agreed with me, but it made Alyssa wonder, "So, you're going to go alone?"

I didn't hesitate.

"I think it would be best."

"What? Dressed as Stephen?" Emily asked.

"No, just, as myself?"

"That's not a good idea, Jack," Ammon said. "I mean, if this is someone who is involved in his murder, won't they be dangerous?"

"If they're involved, shouldn't they know Stephen is dead?" I asked.

Ammon made a face, but decided to back off. Alyssa wasn't having it, though.

"Jack, I think you're right, that if we were to call the police and have them investigate, they'd roll up with tons of cop cars wailing their sirens and flashing their lights all over like a drugged up rave. But we need to have a better plan."

I gave Alyssa a light smile and said, "Okay, how about…"

"We drop you off, and you call the detectives to come as backup. Tell them you have a new lead, but it may be dangerous so you need their help."

Emily and Ammon nodded in agreement with the plan, so I nodded and said, "Yeah, you're right. That's not a bad idea."

I lifted Stephen's tablet up and turned the screen back on. I texted, "Yes, we're meeting tonight. Remind me where?"

Kik showed that the message was read almost instantly, and the person replied, "Evanston Docks. That's where you suggested. North side of the unfinished warehouse."

"I don't think it's a woman," Emily commented.

"It's quite an unflattering place to meet if it is," I said. "But I just want to meet them to see if there's any more information we can scrounge up. And I have a feeling there is plenty more that we haven't discovered yet."

I texted back and said, "Just wanted to make sure. 7 p.m. I'll be there."

"What if they had specified a different time?" Alyssa asked.

"Well, too late now."

The phone buzzed and the response simply said, "K."

"How rude," I muttered.

"Well we have a few hours to prepare, and the Evanston Docks are fairly close to here."

"Do you mind dropping me off or should I take a cab?" I asked Ammon.

"Sure, we can take my car."

"Great. I think I need to take a shower," I said, and I gave Alyssa a kiss on the cheek before I stepped away to the bathroom.

Time for some more answers...

Chapter Fourteen

Seven p.m. rolled around like it had nothing else better to do. After my shower I'd dressed in dark clothes and made sure to drink some caffeine to stay sharp. The only thing I may have forgotten was to wear a diaper, but hopefully it wouldn't come to that.

I didn't want to say I was scared, but based on the meeting area and the secrecy of the messages, I'd say it sounded like a drug deal or something illegal. More importantly, it might be an enemy of Stephen's. Even if it wasn't the killer, I was convinced they'd have more information on what happened to him, or why.

I sat in the back of Ammon's luxurious vehicle with Alyssa at my side and Emily in the passenger seat before me. Alyssa and I were holding hands, and she didn't seem bothered with how sweaty my palms were. Maybe part of the sweat was from hers. I had no idea anymore.

What I did know was that everyone was worried, even Ammon. Not that I thought he wouldn't care, but it was almost like he had some idea as to what this meeting would be about. He knew Stephen better than any of us. And maybe Stephen never gave him specifics, but he knew it was dangerous.

"I'm telling you, Jack, Stephen didn't talk to me about this side of his life, or really any other side beyond school, but this just doesn't sound good," Ammon said.

"Way to build my confidence," I commented.

"I'm just trying to be serious with you. And I want you to be okay, and keep your eyes peeled."

"I gotcha."

"What if this person isn't alone?" Emily questioned.

"Right after I step out of this car, I'm going to call Detective Hannigan and make sure that he and Flores get here ASAP. That way, if it goes south fast, they can hopefully come to my rescue."

I knew Alyssa wasn't comfortable with the whole situation, but she knew that I was going to do it no matter what. There was no stopping me. This was the best lead we had, and after what Lois had talked about with someone harassing Stephen at the beginning of the school year, I wondered if this was our man—or woman.

It was a lead that the police didn't have yet. Because if they knew, wouldn't they pursue it?

Ammon pulled up to the metal playground and loose gravel crunched under his tires.

"I better not leave here with a flat," Ammon said. "You know how these construction sites can be."

I nodded as his car slowed to a stop. Alyssa pulled me in for a kiss, and Emily turned her head awkwardly and wished me luck.

"Lemme call the detectives and let them know I'm here."

I found Hannigan's number and dialed him up. I was sure he'd be thrilled to hear from me.

The phone only rang a few times before he answered.

"I'm sure this is good," he said.

"Right now, I'm at the Evanston Docks about to meet with someone who is really interested in having a chat with him. It's my new lead."

"Jack, what the hell are you doing? You're going to get killed!"

"Well, you and Flores should come on over here and back me up," I said before hanging up the phone.

As Hannigan was probably fuming on the other end of the line, I placed my phone back in my pocket.

"So, how'd the conversation go?" Alyssa asked.

"Oh, they're thrilled. I think you all are good to roll out."

So, the other members of my junior investigative team said their goodbyes and I stepped out onto the cold and damp gravel. Ammon drove off slowly and I tried to get my bearings on the lot.

I stood before the metal playground as the sunshine faded away. There were only a few lights around the docks, but their glow didn't carry at all. The unfinished factory was just metal beams going up, down, and across, with a solid concrete foundation on the ground. I wasn't going to hit my head on any beams, but I might run into one if I wasn't careful.

First order of business: head northeast.

I had my phone on loud and Stephen's tablet on vibrate, but neither of them were in my hands. I was keeping a lookout, just as Ammon had suggested. I was still anxious to meet this person, but I didn't know how they'd react when it was me instead of Stephen. Maybe we could both pass around some information. Maybe he'd gun me down as soon as he saw me. We'd just have to find out.

I continued walking forward, but the walkway started to angle down into the ground. The dip was like a fat "V" with the bottom flattened out. Water and gravel had made its way into the depression and I stepped into one spot where it splashed up onto my jeans.

"This place sucks," I murmured to myself.

The farther I walked into the warehouse, the more boxes and crates were thrown around, stacked by the metal bars going every which way above me and to my sides. They could act as good hiding spots, if this meeting came to that.

I was about to start walking uphill again…

"Stop right there."

The voice was firm and direct. I made sure to stop in my tracks. I didn't hear any accents, any distinguishing sounds in the voice, but I knew it was a man.

"Are you lost?"

"No, I think I'm right where I need to be. Are you lost?" I replied.

"Where's Stephen?"

The man pronounced the "PH" as an F.". Stephen had always pronounced it as a "V".

Anyway, I looked up and the figure above me was completely silhouetted by the backlighting. Plus, he wore a long coat and all dark clothing. There wasn't the sound of a car running behind him and there weren't whispers of other people hanging around, nothing.

"Stephen's dead," I said, bluntly. "But I'm a friend of his, and thought you might be able to answer some questions for me."

"I'm not here to answer questions. I'm here to get the files."

Huh?

"What files?"

Showing my ignorance was the biggest mistake I could've made.

"So you're not even a backup to him?"

"A backup? No, I'm just a friend, like I said before."

There was a long sigh from the shadowed figure, and then he fumed while saying, "You have a lot of nerve coming here."

"I just need answers. I need to know who killed Stephen and I wanted you to help me."

"You're heading down a one-way street with a dead end, my friend."

"It doesn't have to end that way," I said, trying to sound confident.

In a tense situation, you never know what the next sound or action is going to be. I mean, that's what makes it so tense. But I had no idea that my cell phone was going to start ringing with the stupid generic ringtone that I had never gotten around to changing.

"I'm pretty sure it's my mom. I'll call her back," I said as the ringtone continued.

"No, I'm not so sure you will be able to."

A blinding light stabbed right into my eyes and a deafening pop filled the area. I stumbled to the right with my arm up over my eyes and caught a glimpse of the figure holding a pistol with an LED attached to one end. The light started to follow me and I heard another shot. This one landed closer and I felt gravel fly up onto my leg. The pistol was a high caliber, maybe even a fifty caliber. That's when my legs really started moving and I ran sideways.

The pistol kept firing, each shot only slightly fainter than the last. Some hit near me while some were completely off target or stopped by the metal beams. When he reached the end of his clip, he stepped down and started making his way towards me. The figure now looked like a large blob of blinding light. My head hurt and my ears were ringing. I kept blinking, trying to adjust my eyes as I ran as low as I could in the metal jungle.

Who was this guy? What files was he looking for?

My brain gave me a good kick so I could focus more on staying alive as I slowed down and tried to stay as quiet as possible. The man was standing where I had been, maybe twenty-five or thirty yards away. He lowered the pistol, but it didn't do much to show off any of his other features. As I said, he was tall and lean, but his clothes were baggy and long. I had no idea what his face looked like, or anything else.

I glanced around, knowing that if the pistol was high caliber, hiding behind boxes and crates wouldn't help me. Even a low caliber round could pierce through this crap.

I tried steadying my breath; tried to calm down; tried to stay quiet. But it was near impossible. Donovan had shot me a year ago, but I never saw that coming. This situation was different. I knew it was possible, and that panicked me more.

I wasn't even thinking about my phone when it beeped to signify I had a voicemail. I deduced that the noise had given my position away when I saw the bright LED wave its way over to where I was hiding and the gunshots began again.

I dove behind a different set of boxes and watched as my last position was ripped apart, with cardboard and dust dancing about. My attacker's footsteps grew louder as he ran towards my position. I knew I needed to get outside, out in the open, back in the light. The question was, did I want him to waste all of his ammo first or not give him that many chances?

I stood up from the gravel and made my way back to where I'd been before, except a little farther north this time. When I was about halfway over, I saw the light bounce around from where I had been hiding earlier. The shooter examined the damage he'd made, knowing that he could have hit me. He cursed to himself as his head twisted and turned, looking for any signs of my presence.

I made my way west, to the other side of the unfinished warehouse, walking through the opening where I'd once stood. When I was behind some fresh boxes, I pulled my phone out and turned it down all the way. The missed call was from my mom. Thanks again, Mom.

I put my phone away, but some gravel from my hand fell into my pocket as well. I peeked over to see if the man was ready to give up.

The LED bounced around as the man held the pistol at his side. He wanted to kill me. I knew that. He was determined to do so. And it made me wonder, if Stephen weren't already dead, would this man have done it himself?

"I can tell you're just a kid," the man called out, obviously angry. "But you know too much. I have to kill you. For my protection. For my people's protection. So come on out. If you call the police now, it'll take them fifteen minutes to get here, trust me. We know that. Why do you think Stephen and I chose this spot?"

His voice was getting closer. He was walking diagonally through the beams trying to make up time. I thought about how the gravel might've left him a trail. A trail leading right to me.

Y'know, none of this seems like a good idea anymore…

Okay, Jack, now it's time to choose: fight or flight.

I checked around and saw a loose section of rebar. It was long enough so we didn't have to be face-to-face, but short enough that close quarters would be a necessity.

I picked it up silently from the ground and heard his footsteps growing nearer. I could feel my heart in my head as I prepared to strike.

Suddenly, he was a few steps away to my side.

Before he could turn and face me, I rushed at him with the rebar and swung it as hard as I could at the back of his bald head. Unintentionally, I let out a war cry as I made the swing. He turned to look at me, but didn't have time to raise the pistol. Without giving him any time to react, I smacked the side of his face with the rebar and he went down, still conscious but definitely frazzled. I dropped the last minute weapon and bolted the other way as he hit the ground, now firing blindly.

I never said I knew Kung-Fu or anything. I just knew that metal bar plus head equals mild discomfort.

His bullets were hitting all over the place as he fired in a blind rage. I decided that it was my cue to run all the way over to the west side of the warehouse and look for help. The detectives had to be close. I didn't know how much time had passed, but it felt like enough for them to get there.

As I made my way to the other end of the warehouse, I felt like my legs could collapse out from under me. The fear and stress of the running around had really made me feel like putty.

The howling of sirens and the flashing red and blue lights brought me immediate comfort.

Chapter Fifteen

In a matter of seconds, I was surrounded on all sides by regular police cars and unmarked vehicles as well. As I said before, I felt relieved. Here were the cops, ready to save the day and make everything safe.

"Get down on the ground with your hands on your head. Now!"

The order came from one of the officers who were piling out of their vehicles—pistols aimed at me. I complied immediately and dropped to my knees. *Talk about going from serenity to paranoia all over again.*

"No, wait, that's our idiot."

What a flattering nickname.

I heard Flores' voice call out behind the other officers and they started lowering their weapons. She and Hannigan popped out from behind the barricade of cops and she asked, "Where's your lead?"

"I hit him in the head with a piece of rebar," I said, as I pointed back towards the unfinished warehouse. "But he has a high caliber pistol. Maybe a Desert Eagle."

Another man in a suit stepped up behind Flores and Hannigan, pointed towards the warehouse and shouted, "Search parties, go and find this son of a bitch."

"Did you bring the FBI in?" I asked as I settled down.

"No, this is Inspector McTavish," Hannigan explained.

"Yeah, and from what Hannigan and Flores have told me, I don't want you pulling the same bullshit here in my jurisdiction."

"Oh," I said, realizing we were outside of Hannigan and Flores' area.

"Yeah, 'Oh' is right," he said with a mix of Irish in his Boston accent. "Don't let me find you over in my neck of the woods again; you hear me?"

The fierce red-haired McTavish waved his finger in my face and I nodded. When he was satisfied with my response, he ripped his revolver from its holster and ran towards the warehouse. That left me alone with the detectives.

"So, drinks are on you guys? 'Great job, Jack, for finding the real killer?' Nothing?"

"You're underage," Hannigan said.

"Yeah, well, I like mozzarella sticks, too, or a nice bowl of hummus," I said.

"I wish I could legally beat the shit out of you," Flores seethed.

"I'll ignore the obvious threat, but is it because I proved you wrong? That Derrick Martin is not the killer?"

"This doesn't mean anything, Jack!" Flores shouted. "This means that Stephen has other enemies. It means there are other people who may have wanted him dead! This doesn't mean that you found the real killer because the real killer is Derrick Martin."

"And you base that on some steamy story that you heard in a Lifetime Original Film?" I argued.

"We base our findings on facts, Jack. Have you forgotten that? Does your school not teach that? Do they tell you to base them on gut feelings and personal intuition? Because that's not how it works out here, Jack. Not every case that you come across is going to be a family friend or a high school friend who's dead. Do you understand that? Stephen Donahue isn't our only case. We work four or five cases at a time between the two of us. If you think it's just one case at a time, you might want to look into becoming a private eye instead of a detective with the police force, because you're going to be in way over your head."

Flores was done with her rant and I felt like shit. Maybe she was right. Did I only care about these cases because they were personal to me? Would I not care if I was in the police force looking into other cases?

I started to think over the whole thing and wonder if maybe I was overstepping. Well, that was obvious. But maybe there really was no reason to look into this myself.

No, don't give up so easily.

"What did you find on Derrick?" I asked. "You must've found something if you're this convinced."

Flores sighed and a certain sadness filled her eyes. In the end, she didn't like shooting down all my dreams and aspirations, but she said what needed to be said.

"Is your car here?"

"No, my crew dropped me off," I replied.

"Get in our car. We'll take you to the station," Flores said.

"As someone who's under arrest?"

Hannigan scoffed and said, "No... how about, as an annoying

understudy?"

*****

We drove to the station in silence, except for the random outbursts from the police radio. Hannigan turned it down and watched out for anyone crazy on the road. Flores didn't seem very energized about the whole situation. And then there was me, sitting in the backseat sulking about everything, wondering if I had just made a complete fool of myself.

"Flores," she said directly as she answered a phone call.

I heard someone's voice clattering on the other end, and she said, "No sign of the perp?... Yeah, we can get a statement from Jack on what happened.... Okay, see ya, McTavish."

"They didn't find him?" I asked as she hung up the phone.

"Nope."

"Are you making all of this up, Jack?" Hannigan said with a slight smile.

"No, he's not. They found bullet casings and fragments from the bullets, but not the guy," Flores said.

"Was it a fifty caliber?" I asked.

Flores nodded and Hannigan made a face.

"Man, you sure lucked out not getting hit with one of those," he said, as he slowed for a stoplight.

"I know."

Flores finally turned around to face me head on. Her voice changed and had a more motherly tone as she said, "Jack, I know what I said earlier was disheartening, but you'll see soon why we don't need you snooping around and almost getting killed, okay?"

I nodded, hoping she was right; hoping they could give me something that would make me stop looking. Then, I could go home with Alyssa and Emily and be able to relax, finally. And we could stop taking up space at Ammon's apartment.

Hannigan pulled the car around behind the police station and scanned a badge to open the gate. Once we pulled in and parked at the nearest spot, the gate closed and we were locked in.

"Stay close to us, Jack," Hannigan said as we piled out of the car.

This was the part of the station I wasn't supposed to go through unless I was employed there or in deep shit. I followed Hannigan and Flores closely as other cops pulled into the parking lot to call it a night, or left to start their shifts. Hannigan scanned a separate badge for the glass doors and they slid open in opposite directions. Flores and Hannigan led the way as I followed behind them. There were a few awkward stares here and there from the rest of the staff, but they didn't seem that bothered. As long as I wasn't there raising money for a fundraiser, they didn't seem to care.

"What are you hoping to show me?" I asked.

"Evidence," Flores replied.

"I'm anxious to see it."

Flores was the one to scan her badge this time and we stepped down into a concrete stairwell. After going down one floor, we entered a new hallway. She scanned us into a strange and musky room with shelves as high as the ceiling, and I knew this is where the jackpot evidence was.

"Donahue," Hannigan muttered as he looked over all the boxes.

"After we brought Derrick in, we obtained the search warrant to check out his house. It's a nice place, has plenty of hiding spots. But look what the idiot put in his sock drawer?"

After Flores' set up, Hannigan found the right box and placed it on the ground. I stood beside her and waited for Hannigan to show me the amazing piece of evidence, but I had a feeling I knew what it was.

"Okay, Jack, here's juicy piece of evidence number one, the murder weapon."

Hannigan pulled out the clear bag and the silenced pistol dangled in the air. Flores watched as the frown swept over my face. But then, my questions started flooding in.

"So his fingerprints are on it?" I asked.

Hannigan shook his head.

"He wore gloves."

"And you found the gloves?"

Flores sighed and Hannigan joined her off tempo.

"No, we didn't find the gloves—yet. But we have more evidence that we can show you since we knew you wouldn't be satisfied."

Hannigan placed the gun back into the box and lifted it onto the shelf. Then they both led me out of there and back into the stairwell. Our footsteps echoed for an eternity as we made our way to the second floor this time. Coming in from the stairwell, I saw a different environment that looked similar to the police station in Stanton, only slightly larger. Random desks were strewn about with stacks of papers, files, and other office condiments. Flores continued walking until she reached one of the private offices along the wall.

"No, I don't have an office, but we can remote into my PC from this one so we can show you the footage in private," Flores explained.

I thought about mentioning that Lewis had already shown me the footage, which led to investigating the janitor, but I didn't want to get him in trouble.

But when Flores was finished remoting into her PC, I knew the footage was different, because it started a few minutes before the murder. They didn't morph the videos of the different camera angles into one video to show how the events played out like Lewis did. They only had the footage above Stephen's entrance.

"So, there's no reason to watch the catwalk footage because it doesn't show anything of importance," Flores explained. "But pretty soon after Mr. Donahue arrives, you'll see that Derrick Martin comes up to the dean's office from the front and goes on in."

The front view was pretty clear and it showed Derrick walk into camera range from the other end. But the black and white camera angle in front of Stephen's office was strange; strange in the way it only showed the entrance. And the angle was even worse to the point where I could see whoever might be standing in the doorway, but nothing farther than that. Nothing to the left, not the catwalk entrances, nothing. But they were right. There was Derrick Martin, walking up to the office doors, not hiding his face or anything. He stepped into the office, not holding back for the confrontation.

"Of course, as you probably know, there isn't a camera in the dean's office," Hannigan said.

Flores clicked to fast forward just a bit and then said, "But as you can see here, Derrick walks back out of the office, obviously upset and irritated."

"I'm not sure I need a narrator for his emotional state," I said.

Flores shot me a look, but it came off as playful instead of mean. They were happy. They were convinced they'd found the killer, and that it was Derrick Martin: the businessman with so much to lose, and very little to gain from the murder.

Flores clicked to fast forward the tape some more and said, "And once again, here he is, coming to finish the job."

Derrick Martin was now wearing a hoodie, gloves, and had the pistol down at his side. It was hard to tell what kind of clothing he was wearing, but it looked the same as what he had worn before. I was just trying to make sense of it all.

"I think you know the rest. But he shoots him, comes back out, and disappears through the front."

Flores went ahead and closed out of the video and followed up with, "So have we convinced you?"

"With that camera angle," I started, "you can't tell which way he escapes. Isn't there another angle?"

"No. Lewis, the village idiot, and the rest of their security team decided to try and go digital right at the end of the year. So more than half of their cameras were shut off or had run out of tape. This video footage and the catwalk are all we have."

The fact that there weren't any more camera angles was frustrating, to say the least. However, I knew Lewis wasn't an idiot.

"Jack, you just saw this with your very own eyes. I don't think we need to paint this picture anymore for you. And, CSI teams were able to support our theory based on their findings."

"That Derrick Martin walked in to have an initial friendly talk, changed clothes in about three minutes, and then came back to blow him away?" I asked with an obviously uncertain tone.

"Yes, Jack. Maybe Mr. Martin wanted to try and have a friendly confrontation with Mr. Donahue, but when that didn't work he was prepared to end it all. Who knows, that's for the DA and the ADA to figure out. Or to explain to the jury, at least."

Flores finished her explanations and I saw that Hannigan had no strength in him to even try and convince me otherwise. This was supposed to be it. This was their case: a crime of passion.

I knew it was time, though. They had gone out of their way to show me all of the evidence they had, and they didn't even have any obligation to do so. Besides me being annoying, of course.

"Okay, thank you for all of this; I appreciate it," I said, deciding to paint on a convinced face.

"You're convinced?" Flores asked.

"Mostly beyond a reasonable doubt," I said, not wanting to completely lie. "But I see why I need to stay out of it. I don't really want to get shot at again. I think my heart is just now starting to come down from it."

Hannigan laughed softly and said, "Yeah, it's a thrill, all right."

"Oh, speaking of that," Flores said as she sat down behind the computer and took a notepad out of the drawer. "How about you give us a statement of what happened at the docks and then we'll let you go on your merry way?"

Chapter Sixteen

Late Sunday Night

Before I told Flores and Hannigan exactly what had happened, I texted Alyssa to say I was almost finished. At the end of my explanation of the exciting events, Flores and Hannigan offered me a ride back to Ammon's apartment. I declined, saying that my girlfriend was coming to pick me up. And boy, I couldn't wait for them to get me.

"Is she impressed at your detective skills?" Hannigan asked.

"Impressed by or irritated by, not sure," I replied as they walked me out.

"I know how I would feel," Flores said.

The only thing more confusing than Flores' attitude changes over the last two hours was the case at hand. (But, I'll hold the rest of my thoughts till I get in the car with Ammon, Alyssa, and Emily.)

The three of us stepped outside and I saw Ammon's car waiting in front. An officer was about to approach the vehicle and order my friends to move, but I told Hannigan and Flores it was my ride.

"Officer Johnson," Hannigan called out. The officer stopped and turned around. "Don't pay them no mind."

The officer gave a friendly salute and stepped away with his cigarette burning in the light wind. I saw Ammon behind the wheel of his BMW with Emily in the passenger's seat and Alyssa waiting for me in the back, as usual. I was happy to see them, but I didn't know how they'd react to the whole "getting shot at" story.

"Mind if we walk you all the way?" Flores asked.

"No, I don't."

I stepped on over to the car and let myself into the back. Ammon rolled the driver's side window all the way down and Flores poked her head in.

"It's nice to meet with Jack's investigative crew again," Flores started. Alyssa grabbed my hand and held it as soon as she could. "But I want to make something clear. The case is closed. We've found video and physical evidence on Derrick Martin, okay? And little Jack Sampson here almost got killed tonight by a lead you guys were trying to pursue."

Alyssa's grip on my hand got tighter and Emily turned to me with a shocked expression.

"So I don't want you four snooping around anymore, okay? As I said, case is closed. Done. No need for further investigation."

"Yes, we understand, loud and clear," Ammon said.

"Thank you, Mr. Samara. And the rest of you?"

Alyssa and Emily nodded and I did a slight nod as well. Flores' eyes swept across the interior of the car one last time, and then she said, "Okay. Now, get on out of here. Get out of town like you were supposed to Friday night. From what the chief told me, you guys missed one hell of a party."

Flores stepped back from the car and Hannigan gave the final wave. Ammon pressed for his windows to roll up slowly and popped his BMW into Drive. We were just about to pull out into the street when Emily asked, "The person you met with almost killed you?"

"Yeah…" I said, with my mind in a different place.

"How?" Alyssa asked.

"He started shooting at me after I said Stephen was dead."

"Are you hurt?" Ammon asked as Emily and Alyssa gasped.

"No, he wasn't a very good shot. Plus, I haven't even told you guys about how I got to hit him upside the head with a piece of rebar."

"Jesus Christ, Jack!" Alyssa said, holding my hand with a death grip.

"It's okay. I'm still here, with no extra holes."

"Yeah, but…"

Emily interrupted, "But, it wasn't the killer? They say Derrick Martin is?"

"That's what their evidence proves. They claim whoever I met was just another enemy of Stephen's."

"I didn't think Stephen had any enemies," Ammon muttered.

"Yeah, well, Lois wanted to make sure that I didn't idolize Stephen."

I shook my head as the footage played over and over in my head, with all of the blind spots and shitty angles. Everything the man had said to me before opening fire on me, something about files—*what the hell was he talking about?*

"Jack, I know you have plenty of reasons to not look okay, but you really look bad," Alyssa said.

I felt as if I was in front of an audience in olden days when they'd get ready to throw rotten vegetables at me for what I was about to say.

"I know they found the gun at Derrick's house, and they have footage of him going in to talk to Stephen, and then he comes back three minutes later in a different outfit with his face hidden to kill him, but… that doesn't really make sense to me. It just doesn't add up."

"Jack, maybe you've done all that you can do. The police seem pretty convinced that they have the right guy. And they're professionals! They went to school for this, and it's not their first case," Alyssa said.

She sighed loudly as she noticed that I was getting irritated. The rest of the car ride was silent, except in my mind. It was running around like a three-ring circus. Different theories and ideas were popping into my head, nonstop. *Who was the silhouetted man with a gun? Did I even see his face at all? Would I recognize him if I saw him again?*

The moment right as I hit him in the face with the rebar kept replaying. I felt like he had darker skin—but I had no idea what nationality he was.

And the files… what files? Why would I be a backup to Stephen? What was he talking about?

Before I knew it, we were back at the apartment in the underground parking garage and Ammon and Emily were climbing out of the car.

"Hey, Jack, are you coming?"

I looked up at Emily and Ammon as they waited for me, then I turned to Alyssa. She wasn't smiling or anything, just very blank-faced. The sight made me feel sad for giving everyone the silent treatment, but then she said, "Mind if we have your keys? I want to talk to Jack alone. We won't drive off or anything."

Ammon didn't linger. He pulled out his ring and detached the car key.

"When you come up to the apartment, just knock. We'll let you in."

Even though I knew we were still in Ammon's car to have a private conversation, I still felt that warm feeling flush over my body. I decided to make a joke before I blushed too much.

"We can find other places to make out, you know," I said.

She knew, based on my delivery, that I wanted to lighten the mood. It wouldn't work this time.

"Jack, we need to talk about all of this."

"About us?"

"No, this case."

"What about it?"

"You were shot at. You could have been killed."

"Do you think that never happens out there with detectives when they're on the job?"

"Yeah, but you're not…"

Alyssa stopped herself. I didn't take offense to what she was about to say, but she tried to cover her tracks anyway.

"You're not on the job. You're not obligated to solve this case. You haven't taken that oath yet. And yet, you still feel like you have to for whatever reason."

I was staring deep into Alyssa's eyes, as if I was about to tell her I loved her for the very first time.

"But that's the problem. No matter what the police tell me, no matter what evidence they throw my way, I'm not satisfied. I think I want to be. I know that I just want to be back in Stanton with you and everyone else, and wish that we hadn't missed the party. But there's something inside of me, something deep that I can't even understand or comprehend, that is driving me farther and farther into this case, trying to uncover that final piece that I know still exists. It's not open and shut."

"You almost died, Jack!"

"Yeah, to find out the real reason why someone else did!"

Alyssa's face was tense and I knew that she was holding back tears. She was scared of how far I was willing to go. And honestly, there was nothing in my mind saying, "Hey, idiot, stop while you're ahead".

"Baby, I'm sorry..."

Alyssa wiped at her face and she said, "I don't think I get mad at you because I think you're wrong. It's because I know you're right."

"Right about what?"

"I don't feel like Derrick killed Stephen either. They were too good friends. Ammon and Emily said they'd go out for drinks all the time. They'd see each other on the holidays. Even if Stephen banged Alicia, Derrick had no reason to go take his vengeance that far."

"Banged? Really?" I said with a half-smile.

"Just wanted to catch you off guard. You're not the only funny person here."

She came in for a kiss and I gladly accepted it. All of this love and support from her... I couldn't imagine what I'd do without it.

Once the kiss ended and our eyes began to open, like two bear cubs coming out of hibernation, I said, "So, we should search Stephen's house, right?"

Alyssa kept a serious face and said, "Ask yourself this, Mr. Sampson. What is it about this case that bugs you the most?"

I made a face at her. Not that it was a bad question or anything, just seemed to be as simple as someone losing their keys and you ask them "Well, where's the last place you put them?"

"Honestly? Besides Derrick Martin not seeming like the murderous type, and besides… well, practically everything else? I feel like the security footage just doesn't make sense. The footage they showed me has too many blind spots.

"Then we should go see Lewis tomorrow," Alyssa said. "He'll help us, I'm sure."

"That's a good idea," I said, not really sure what we'd find at Stephen's house anyway… beside a nice supply of condoms.

"Let's head upstairs before Ammon and Emily start thinking we're up to no good," Alyssa said as she reached for the door.

It might be the fact that I was still a teenager, or from all of the other excitement the day had to offer, but I grabbed Alyssa's hand at the door handle and said, "Or, we could let them think something bad *is* going on…"

Alyssa did an exaggerated "Ooo" and I scooted up next to her. My right hand went behind her lower back and my left hand went up to gently hold her face in place. I still saw a faint tremor in her lower lip as I went in for a kiss and we forgot about everything for a while.

Chapter Seventeen

Mid-day on Monday

My head was pounding from staying up too late the night before, wondering about the security footage. Would Lewis even be able to provide anything extra? Or would we be able to find anything at all? Alyssa convinced me that the school was a better option, and I agreed with her. But what else could we uncover that we hadn't before?

It was only me, Alyssa, and Emily on the prowl to the school. Ammon had left sometime after Alyssa and I came back from the BMW with the excuse that his parents had flown into town to surprise him.

"His parents are weird," Emily said.

"Have you met them?" I asked as we piled into my car.

"No, but I'm pretty sure I don't want to. They surprised him one other time. I think it was fall break. They like for him to go to the hotel and stay the night with them. Some family tradition that they practice."

"Maybe they just miss their son," I sympathized.

"I guess. But I'd feel weird cramming into a hotel room with my parents when I'm twenty-five."

I had the drive to the school memorized. It only took me one or two times to do that with a route, unless you threw me into a hedgerow maze. Then it might take me three times. Hah.

I parked in the same relative spot as I had a million times. We all piled out and made our way into the school. Alyssa whipped out her phone as we walked and started texting someone. I decided to act like the worrisome boyfriend and said, "Who are you texting, my dear?"

"Lewis. He's going to meet us over here at the door. They'll be locked by now."

Either Lewis was just passing by the doorway or ran over to it, because we didn't have to wait outside long. He turned a few bolts and pushed the door out towards us.

"The trio has arrived once again," he said.

We stepped past him and he followed us up to Stephen's office. I knew the walk must be a painful one to Emily and Alyssa, but I hoped they were okay with it. I was pretty sure they were going to finish their degrees at this school and not change just because of what happened. But if they did change schools, I wouldn't blame them.

Stepping into the office, we saw that no one had straightened up the mess the police had made scrounging for clues. A part of me wondered why we were there, but Alyssa made it apparent.

"Ugh, I forgot they took his computer... shit."

"Aren't we here for the security footage anyway?" I asked.

"Yeah, that's your job. But I was thinking last night..."

"Thinking? Alone? Aren't we a team?" I asked, acting offended.

"No," Alyssa said with a wink.

You are so bad...

"What footage do you want?" Lewis asked.

"If you have any footage of sophomores taking their finals with a clear view over their shoulders, I'm sure they would appreciate it," I said.

Lewis gave me a stifled laugh and Emily clapped her hands once.

"What? Is there a fly?" I asked.

"No. Lewis, before you get the footage that you gave the police, can you take us to the library?"

"I don't really want to do this much walking today," Lewis said as he left the office.

We followed behind him and took the center catwalk to the (you guessed it) center building. As much as I hated the layout of the school, I'm sure Lewis hated it just as much, if not more. I mean, he worked here. Actually, I was leaning more towards the idea that he *lived* here.

Once we arrived at the middle building, he took us downstairs to the library and unlocked the glass doors. He stepped aside as he held the door for us and said, "Can I trust the three of you in here while I go grab the footage? What do you want it on, a USB?"

"Yeah, if you have an extra one. Sorry, I didn't bring one," I said.

"Oh yeah, I have plenty. Just stay in here till I come back, please."

"We won't make ourselves a security concern, don't you worry."

Lewis gave me one last look before he closed the library door behind him and left us alone.

"Did you forget to return a book?" I asked.

"Jesus, Jack, you're on a roll," Alyssa said without much enthusiasm.

I decided to pipe down as Emily made her way over to one of the several dead computers. She sat down in one of the outdated chairs and pulled herself towards the computer to make sure she had good posture. Once she started to log in and type in Stephen's name, I started to pick up on what she was doing.

"I don't know why I didn't think of this last time we were here...but we can use remote log in to get onto his computer."

Alyssa made a face and said, "No we can't."

"Well, not his actual computer and personal files, but we can get into his emails and snoop around there."

That's just what Flores did last night. Duh, the email is on a shared server. Why didn't I think of that?

Emily finished logging in as Stephen and waited for a second to dive into his Outlook. A few small windows popped up showing that we were connecting to all the servers and whatever else, but when they disappeared, Emily clicked Outlook. My heart started to race at the possibility of what we might find.

"Did you check his email constantly?" I asked.

"No," she replied. "Most of the emails I needed to be a part of were CCed to me, or instantly forwarded based on the rules he set. But I forgot that I had his password in my desk for emergencies, and then I thought of the shared server..."

"And then you killed the fly?" I asked.

Emily rolled her eyes and said, "Forgive me for getting excited."

"No, it's okay, this is good. Great idea," I reassured her.

We all glanced over his email at the main inbox. There were a few messages pending to be read. The one we were thrown on to after opening the email was just a "Congrats on another year of teaching" and other crap like that. But taking a look at the left side of his email, he had tons of subfolders with all different categories. There were the basic ones, like IT, Administration, Weekly Announcements, etc., but there was one folder that caught our eyes more so than the rest.

"Does everyone else see the folder that has the little lock on it?" I asked.

Alyssa and Emily nodded, and when Emily clicked on it, the result was less than surprising.

A message popped up that said, "File 5103 is locked. Please enter your password".

"The Windows password, or a new one?" I asked.

Emily looked over a piece of paper she had obtained from her desk and said, "He did put two passwords on here. I doubt it's his Windows password."

She took a shot at putting the other password in and was right on the money. The file opened up like an insecure boy in a middle school counselor's office (not that I'd know anything about that). But the emails only left us with more questions.

"They're all read receipts," Alyssa announced.

"'Email was read by the above recipient on'... and it's all throughout the year. Mainly just a few months ago," Emily muttered as she clicked through the emails."

"Who owns these email addresses?" I asked.

"They're completely random. None of them look the same... Oh, wait, there's one. SAlb127 is a Yahoo! address. It's appeared three times."

I pulled out my phone and pulled up my email.

"And all of the messages Stephen sent just say 'PSA, thank you'. Nothing else."

I wrote a quick email to SAlb127 and sent it off. No fancy message or anything, but what I predicted would happen, happened.

"'Mailer demon, failure to send message. Please make sure you typed in the correct address,'" I read aloud.

"You didn't have to use your email, Jack," Alyssa scolded.

"Oh, good point. Whatever. What are the attachments?"

Emily double-clicked one of the PDF files and I started to wonder if they were nude photos. Which, is kind of dumb, but knowing his lifestyle, nothing was off bets. However, if he did send nudes, he wouldn't make them PDFs—or would he?

They weren't nudes, which I first thought was a good thing. But as we browsed over the information at hand, my mind started racing.

"He was sending off student applications?" Emily asked.

"Not only that, they're applications to this school," Alyssa added.

One of my favorite "w" words danced around in my head and it started to become too much. *Why* would he send student applications to random email addresses? Especially ones that no longer exist.

That's when I noticed Emily had her phone out and she took a picture of the computer screen.

"We need to go back into his office," Emily said as she closed out the email.

Lewis was just about to enter the library when the three of us started to walk past him.

"Well, here's the flash drive for whoever wants it," Lewis said as he held it up in the air.

"I'll take that. Now follow us to the dean's office, please," I said.

"Y'know, how about I go back and eat my lunch. Alyssa, text me when you guys leave and I'll secure the building then," he replied with a sigh.

"Fine by me."

And again, we went up the stairs, over to the catwalk doorway, across the catwalk to the main building, and then over to Stephen's office. I wasn't sure of Emily's reasoning for going to his office again. His computer wasn't there and the discovery we made was on his email, so that meant...

"Mind narrating this journey?" I asked.

"I just want to check one other thing."

Emily walked directly into Stephen's office and stepped over to the file cabinet along the left wall. Alyssa flipped on the light switch for her and I stayed in the doorway. Emily dug around in the file cabinet, silent and determined. I was excited to see what she would come up with. I was glad that we were all just as invested in this as the next person.

"Here," Emily muttered.

She pulled out a file and showed it to us.

"Okay, so you see how this front cover page has a plastic piece right here on the side? This paper that the school uses for the applications is unreadable to most copiers and scanners. The school bought this scanner especially for the handling of these applications. It's a security measure."

"The paper can't be scanned? Don't they just get the applications off the internet anyway?" I asked.

"No, you must call in or email a request and they mail it to you physically. Then, the students have to mail them back."

"Okay, go on," I said.

"So on that scanner right there, you have to enter this page first to start the scanning process. And as you'll see here, it leaves a tick mark on this plastic every time it's scanned."

Emily showed us the file and we saw the tick marks, plain as day along the side of the paper. It started to look like a comb with small but thick bristles.

"This file has about five tick marks on it, meaning it's been scanned in that many times," Emily explained, and then she lifted up her phone. "The first tick mark was made when it was sent to that random email that we just checked."

"And it wasn't supposed to be sent there first, right?" I asked.

"No, not at all."

"And it's been scanned four extra times after that."

"The most a file should be scanned is maybe once or twice. This file is from two years ago, and it's been scanned five times," Emily said, and she walked over to the file cabinet once more. "In fact, all of these have been scanned multiple times more than they should have been."

"But once the file is scanned and sent off, can't they just print it off? Or view it like we did?" Alyssa asked.

"When we have to send them off for whatever reason, the recipient of the email has to have that software as well, and one of these printers available if they want to do that. Otherwise, when you open that attachment—well, you shouldn't be able to. It's a different kind of PDF, a secure one through this weird and annoying technology. But, Stephen was able to send them as plain PDFs, meaning anyone could read them, print them, whatever. He still had to scan them with this machine, but he was able to convert them afterward."

"That whole process gives me a headache, even though I think I get it," I said. "But you're saying he was sending these applications off to a random person?"

"Applications to random *people*," Emily said, and made the plural form very apparent.

I still had the flash drive in my hand and sweat started to form around it. I looked to Alyssa, who looked at me, and then we looked back at Emily.

"So, what now?" Alyssa asked.

So, I said what was on my mind.

"I need a Big Mac."

Chapter Eighteen

My taste buds were satisfied just moments later as I stuffed the Big Mac into my mouth after dipping it in an embarrassingly massive amount of ketchup. Alyssa and Emily shared a twenty-piece nuggets and some fries. Little kids ran past us constantly as the parents allowed them to go into the playground area. I don't know why the parents acted like it was only a maybe that they would be allowed to go into the play area. I guess that was to get them to eat their food. Oh, the joys of parenting.

I was about to finish my French fries when Alyssa asked, "Okay, so... now do you have an answer?"

"About the emails?" I asked. They both nodded, and I reached for a napkin to wipe my mouth. "I really don't know. I mean, Emily here said there was no reason to send them to random people, right?"

"Definitely not Yahoo! and Gmail accounts. It should have strictly been people from the school or maybe outside police stations for background checks."

"Hmph," I said throwing another fry into my mouth. "No, I can't really think of a reason to send out student applications to random email addresses with nothing more than a 'PSA, thank you.'"

"Well, when in doubt, Google it," Alyssa said.

"You Google it."

"What did you say?"

Alyssa tried to look angry, but I knew she was kidding around.

"Yes, dear," I said, acting scared.

"That's what I thought."

I stuck my tongue out quickly and filled in the search bar: Dean of Admissions sending student applications...

Sometimes, it was horrifying to see what Google auto-filled for you when you were searching, especially when it was accurate. This was definitely one of those moments.

I looked up at Alyssa and Emily after searching the top result.

"One of the top search results is: Dean of Admissions sending student applications to terrorist groups."

A knot formed in my stomach, and based on Emily and Alyssa's grimaces, they were experiencing the same feeling. Not just from the greasy food, but from the thought of this being the truth to what Stephen was doing.

"What? Are you joking?" Alyssa asked.

"Not at all," I replied.

There was a story from a local news station somewhere in Pennsylvania about a dean of admissions sending off student applications to foreign aggressors to score some cash. The next story I found was the same but in Long Island.

"There are a few stories popping up about deans sending the applications off so terrorists all around the world could use the information to make fake IDs so they could gain entry to the United States..."

"What!" Emily objected.

Alyssa whipped out her phone and started Google searching as well. Emily leaned over to look at Alyssa's phone and they both skimmed the news stories in shock.

"This guy in Pennsylvania, he made just under a million dollars on all the info he was sending," Alyssa said.

"Were there any other search results besides this?" Emily asked.

I shook my head, and it started to turn hot. My rage was starting to build and I couldn't slow it down.

"I can't believe it."

"We shouldn't believe it. Stephen wouldn't do that," Emily argued.

"Why else would he send these out? He had no other reason. It makes so much sense. The terrorists would make email addresses, he'd send the applications off, and then they'd delete the addresses. They're trying to cover their tracks.'"

"But there would still be ways to find these people," Alyssa urged.

"I just can't believe it. I can't believe he was supplying this information to the same people my father was fighting over there. Some friend, he's aiding those who killed him!"

My outburst made my face flush over and I knew I was redder than a tomato. I immediately felt embarrassed. Alyssa stood up from the clunky booth and came to sit by me. She slowly reached her arms around me and said, "Hey, hey, Jack, it's okay. We're here for you."

I looked over Alyssa's shoulder, that my face was buried in, and saw the other people in the restaurant turn away. The invisible steam left my ears and I felt calm again. Well, semi-calm. The idea that Stephen might have spoon-fed information to different terrorist organizations...

Alyssa remained sitting beside me in the clunky plastic booth to sooth me, and Emily gave me a whispered smile. Their combined love helped me cool down.

"So, that would make more sense about that the guy who met you—he must have been a terrorist," Alyssa said, piecing it all together.

"And I know too much," I said.

"That seems to be the case most of the time," Emily joked.

"I would have to agree with both of you. I mean, that's the only logical conclusion: he was a terrorist who didn't receive the files, or he was at the wrong after-hours shooting range."

"But he didn't know that Stephen was dead. And since Derrick had the murder weapon at his house..."

Emily stopped short and I started to wonder as well. *The man who attacked me wasn't the killer; that much was clear—unless Derrick was working with him?*

"I don't know. Killing Stephen over infidelity or killing him over knowing too much about their operation. Both sound possible, but which one is more likely?" I asked.

Not too long after we finished our meals, we left the McDonald's. Alyssa was fascinated by all of the stories popping up on her Google search that had to do with college administrations handing out files of their own prospective students.

"I knew identity theft was more than posing as someone with their credit card, but this is just incredible," Alyssa said. "Giving the information to terrorists, ex-cons, basically anyone who needs a new life."

"Or someone's life to *hide* under," I commented.

I felt my phone start to buzz in my front left pocket. I was about to reach for it, but that was a big no-no to Alyssa. To my surprise, she reached over and began fiddling with my pocket to retrieve my phone. I squirmed a little, but she mouthed "It's the chief," and answered the call for me.

"Hey, Chief," I started.

With a laugh, Alyssa pointed over to a parking spot next to the curb and I pulled over. Safety first, kids. I mean, I honestly would have kept driving around, but I knew this conversation would take a little more brain power than just saying to my mom that I was okay over and over again.

"Jack, I don't know how closely you're following up on the case," Chief

Ramzorin said.

"I think that's the whole reason we're still out here. Why? What's up?"

"Derrick's arraignment is tomorrow. I don't mean to scare you or force your investigation, but you need to really crack down on whatever leads you might have if you think Derrick is innocent."

"We have some uncut video footage from the school grounds. I'm hoping that will lead us somewhere. The police showed me the video they've cut together for a trial, but not the separate feeds," I explained.

"I've also heard the video footage may not be very reliable."

"You heard that, or you know that?"

Chief Ramzorin laughed lightly on the other end.

"Well, Jack, you piqued my interest in this case, what can I say?"

"I don't think you're the only one," I replied.

"I'm sure you have plenty more to do, so I'll let you go. Don't stay out there all summer, okay?"

"I don't know, this is kind of a cool town," I said, but Alyssa and Emily were shaking their heads in disbelief.

"Okay, well I hope to see you back here soon. And remember what I said, Jack."

Just remember—sometimes, two shaded figures can look very similar to one another, eh?

"I remember. See you sooner than later, Chief."

Chapter Nineteen

We were back at Ammon's apartment for however long we needed to be. I hated staying inside so much with how nice it was outside, but there was no time to waste. I had been fighting this crazy desire to watch the footage over and over again, even though I didn't have the footage. Until now.

Emily plopped down on the couch and I asked Alyssa if I could borrow her laptop.

"Damn, it's dead. You can still use it, just stay close to the wall."

"No problem, sweet pea."

She didn't laugh and neither did I. At this point, my smart-assery was never going to stop. I couldn't tell if it was a curse or something far worse.

The couch was too far away from the electrical outlet, so I pulled a lightweight love seat over and sat down. Fighting with the ridiculously tangled charging cable, I managed to get everything plugged in and get the power flowing. I had the flash drive already plugged in so when the computer started coming up, the white flash drive blinked red five times through the plastic and I knew it was being read. But then, the dreaded password prompt came up.

"Alyssa, honey, what's your password?" I asked.

"I think you know it!" she mocked from the kitchen.

I typed in what I thought it was and the invalid password prompt came up.

"It's not: IluvJackSampson2013."

"Oh, no, I changed it to: LeoDicaprioforlife2822."

"How dare you."

Alyssa came over to me with a smile and said, "Okay, hand it over."

"You don't want to tell me your password?"

"Not out loud. It's very cryptic. I'd sound weird."

This time I didn't comment any further. I just stared at the side of Alyssa's right eye as she leaned over and typed the password in for me. It only took her maybe two seconds, even though the password seemed to be sixteen characters long.

My girl is a dork.

"Done."

We smiled at each other for a moment, but she eventually walked away. I wished we were at one of our houses together, holding each other, not having a care in the world, except for each other.

No time for all of that gushy shit.

The computer took about a minute to be fully ready for some serious clicking. I jumped into the Start Menu, then Computer, and then the flash drive. I was a little surprised, and disappointed, that Lewis hadn't left anything else on the flash drive. It was a brand new one. What did I wish was also on there? I don't know—Lewis singing in the shower? I mean, with the camera outside of the shower…no nudity. Whatever. You get what I mean.

I started playing the first video named *Front Camera 1*. It was that terrible angle adjacent to Stephen's office door. Sure, I could see Derrick Martin clear as day walk into the office with a little bit of fire in his step, but a wider angle would've been so much nicer.

I exited out of that one and double-clicked on the next one, *Northwest Catwalk*. Lewis had set up both videos to show three hours of footage, from 5:30, when most students were clearing out, till 8:30 when the police finally came in to see Stephen's lifeless body. Footage from the office would have helped, but you get what you can.

The catwalk footage didn't show anything new, either. Just the footage of the janitor going to the restroom—that I thought was incriminating—but ended up being a farce. Something about both videos bothered me though. It wasn't the camera angles; I had to deal with that no matter what. It wasn't the lighting or lack of sound; those wouldn't help much. What about this scenario was bothering me? If it wasn't Derrick who killed Stephen, why couldn't I think of that one thing that would prove him to be innocent?

"Jack, when we get back to Stanton, I need to buy some new shoes. These are not good for investigating crimes," Emily whined as she pulled her Toms off.

"New shoes?" I said, mostly focused on the computer.

But her words hit me in a way that they shouldn't have in any regular conversation.

New shoes?

Shoes…. feet… smelly… No, wrong way, come back… shoes… feet… hands… gloves… fingers… indentifiers…

That's when it hit me.

"Footprints!" I shouted.

"Huh?" Emily and Alyssa said in unison.

"If Derrick isn't the killer, that means—based on the blind spot—both he and the killer would've entered from the front, but one of them escaped a different way. So Derrick's prints would have been the most prevalent in the front area."

My blood was pumping so fast. I was so focused. I loved this feeling—even though it was inadvertently caused by a friend's death. I played the footage on *Front Camera 1* and noticed that the catwalk doorway wasn't included in the shot. It was outside of that camera's field of view. That's when I checked the catwalk camera and realized it only covered about 75% of the catwalk. The front doors weren't visible at all.

"Jack, what did you find?" Alyssa asked as she closed in on me.

I looked up with my heart and mind racing and tried to formulate my words.

"Emily, put your torn-up Toms back on. We gotta go back to the school."

*****

Lewis met us at the same doors again, but he wasn't too happy.

"How many damn times are you guys going to come up here?" he asked.

"No time, Little Red," I joked. "Can you go in the surveillance room, or your lair, or whatever the hell you want to call it, and watch the camera from above the catwalk? Let us know when you're there. Call us—I mean—Alyssa. Sorry, my mind is flying!"

I ran past Lewis while Emily and Alyssa tried explaining, but they decided it was better to try and keep up with me. I'd cursed the layout of the school over and over again in the past, but now that I'd been here it so many times, running through it didn't seem as hazardous as I thought it would.

"Jack!" Alyssa yelled.

"Why are we running?" Emily called out.

"I don't know. I'm excited!"

I ran up the stairs and tried stepping up two at a time to make my way to Stephen's office. My middle school gym teacher would have been so proud of me right now, but my leg muscles weren't.

I took a deep breath at the top of the stairs and saw my amazing girlfriend and the equally amazing Emily finally catch up.

"Jack—Jack, what, why," Alyssa huffed and puffed as she finished the last few stairs.

"Hey, we're all pretty fit, for the most part."

"Yeah, well, you must've processed your McDonald's a lot faster than us," Emily groused.

"Hey, can you call Lewis?" I asked.

"Please?" Alyssa replied.

"Yes, please do."

Alyssa called him, but then handed me the phone. I waited for Lewis to answer.

Once he did, he said, "Hey, I don't see you on the catwalk."

"Go to Front Camera 1 real quick if you can," I requested.

"Okay," Lewis replied. "Okay, now I see you and your two girlfriends."

"Great. Okay, so if I walk over here... Let me know when you can't see me anymore."

"You got it."

I walked slowly over towards the catwalk doorway and waited for Lewis to say he couldn't see me. I wasn't even in front of the catwalk when his voice came through the phone, "Okay, you've disappeared."

"Okay, now can you change to the catwalk video feed, please?" I said, with the phone on speaker.

"And...done."

I stepped out into the catwalk and said, "Okay, can you see me?"

"No."

"What about now?" I asked as I kept stepping forward.

"No, you're still in the blind spot."

I sped up my pace and when I was almost halfway down, he said, "Okay, I see you."

"All of me or just the top of my head?" I asked.

"All of you."

I turned to my right, scanning the oblong horizontal windows that lined the wall. Each had two locks at the top. They didn't require keys or anything of the sort. Someone could just grab the latch and pull them. And as I looked over the window in the blind spot, I realized the locks weren't completely pushed back to where they needed to me. I muttered, "Then that must mean..."

What a classic escape method. And, out of sight from the cameras. Always important.

"Jack, what is it?" Alyssa asked.

"Lewis, can you come back to us, if you don't mind?" I asked, and then I hung up the phone.

Alyssa and Emily stared at me with eager eyes, so I had to satisfy them.

"I'm still convinced Derrick Martin did not kill Stephen Donahue. Whoever did kill Stephen entered through the front, just like Derrick, but then escaped through the window, knowing they'd be in the blind spots."

"So that means we can narrow down the killer to someone in the school?" Alyssa asked.

"A student, part of the staff, maybe a security guard..."

"You don't think..." Emily started to say.

"Lewis? No. Although, if he bursts through that door with a gun, I guess we could change that answer," I replied. "But before he does, let's grab some scotch tape from Stephen's office and a blank piece of paper with a limited number of fingerprints on it. And a folder, a pocket folder or a file folder."

We walked together to Stephen's office and Emily stepped over to her desk to grab the roll of scotch tape. I thanked her once she handed it over and I made my way back to the catwalk while they grabbed the other items. When we arrived, Lewis was standing there, fortunately without a gun.

"Find what you were looking for?" he asked.

"Almost. Just one last thing," I said as I unrolled the scotch tape.

First, I made sure to cover both locks with it, then pulled it away and stuck it on the paper. Next, I placed tape all along the underside of where you'd pull up to open the window and stuck that to the paper. Alyssa and Emily stepped up to us with the folder and placed it next to the window I was attending.

"I see plenty of fingerprints on here," I said.

"Y'know, some of those might be mine, but you know that I..."

"Yeah, Lewis, we know. Don't worry," I said.

I took a pen from the janitor's breast pocket and wrote where the fingerprints came from above the respective pieces of tape.

"Maybe I can convince Hannigan that he owes me," I said as I slipped the paper into the file folder.

A familiar ringtone erupted and I turned to Alyssa, who started to take her phone from her pocket.

"Oh, shit. It's my grandparents."

Alyssa stormed away like she was upset, so Emily followed her. I wanted to make sure everything was okay, too, but I had more business to discuss with Lewis.

"Lewis, I really appreciate all of your help, but there's one more thing you could do for me that would make this all so much easier."

"What's that, Jack?" he replied.

"Do you have a camera feed from the parking lot? Or right outside of this catwalk?"

"The one right outside of the catwalk is right here," Lewis said.

He pointed at a metal pole that was barely seen because of the large elm tree that had grown tremendously over its lifetime.

"It can't be reached any longer, and that tree can't be cut down. It'd be too hazardous. We might hurt the catwalk."

"That doesn't answer the question about the parking lot cameras."

For the first time since I had met him, Lewis was hesitant. His reaction made me start to rethink the whole "Lewis isn't involved" theory. But, he had a good explanation. Well, decent.

"I had to do the parking lots first, of course. Otherwise, if someone had a wreck out there and we didn't have footage, we'd have a lot of pissed off people here."

"Yeah, so…"

"But the cops didn't ask for that footage. Just the footage inside the school."

"Why would they not ask for that?"

"Maybe I didn't explain it right when they asked which cameras worked. I thought they just meant *inside*. I'm not a cop!"

"Well neither am I, but you need to give me that footage. It's the last piece to this puzzle."

"But, I didn't give it to the cops."

"Lewis," I started, "this isn't about giving it to me or giving it to the cops. This is about getting down to the truth of what happened to someone that you swore to protect. Or at least, surveil."

"Are you saying this is my fault?" Lewis started to argue.

"No, man, I'm saying, if you give me the footage, the detectives and I can put away the real scumbag who did this. Huh? Doesn't that sound better than locking away a man who didn't do it? Wouldn't your conscience feel better?"

I had hit a nerve with Lewis, but luckily, it was in a good way.

"Alright, alright, let me go down and get it. Do you still have the flash drive or do you need another one?" he asked.

"I left the other one back at the apartment," I said.

"That's fine. I have plenty."

Lewis started to walk off and I said, "Hey, thank you."

"No problem, Jack."

I smiled and my adrenaline rush began to simmer down. Finally, things seemed to be going the way they needed to.

Wait, maybe I should check on Alyssa and Emily…

Chapter Twenty

Seeing your girlfriend, or really any loved one, crying isn't the most comfortable situation. Not for me, anyway. I want to console them and make them feel better, but for me, crying is an emotional shower: it's better to do it alone.

That being said, when I exited the catwalk and saw that Alyssa had just finished crying after being on the phone, I instantly thought the worst had happened.

"Alyssa, hey," I said softly. "What happened?"

Alyssa sniffled and said, "I'm sorry, it's stupid.... My grandparents are just saying I really need to come home, now. No excuses."

"My parents were on the phone, too, and they said the same thing," Emily said, looking about as sad as Alyssa, but without the tears.

"I mean," I started, "I can't blame them for wanting you home. Things are pretty crazy over here."

Alyssa stood up from the stairs and hugged me close. Emily looked away and I gave Alyssa a soft kiss.

"Jack, whatever it is that you found," Alyssa said as she pulled away from me, "how about we just turn it in to the police and get going?"

"Was my mom on the phone, too?" I asked.

"You're supposed to call her," Alyssa said.

"Oh, great..."

But Alyssa wasn't amused, and I realized that I might have ignored her original question. Well, ignored is the wrong word. Let's say, avoided.

"Jack..."

I made a face and sighed lightly, and then tried to explain myself.

"Baby, and Emily, if you have your doubts as well..."

"I don't know how I feel," Emily said.

"Either way, I feel that it would be best if I rode this out till the end. I know I came here because you're not sure about your car, but you can take mine."

"Jack, I'm not worried about my car. I'm worried about you," she replied.

At that moment, Lewis appeared with the new flash drive and gracelessly stepped into the conversation.

"Hey, Jack, uh, here you go. How about you guys just text me when you leave and I'll lock up, okay?"

"I appreciate it," I replied.

Lewis nodded and stepped away. Alyssa grabbed my arm and said, "Jack, I'm not worried about my car. My grandpa changed his mind and wants me to bring it back home anyway. Wants to check it and make sure it doesn't need any crazy repairs. But why do you have to stay here?"

"Do you worry that every detective is like Donovan?" Emily asked.

Just hearing his name made me feel cold. Such an abuse of power, and for what? So his cousin could get away with a pointless murder?

"No, I don't think that. But if we're dealing with a terrorist organization, who knows how many might have infiltrated the police here? I mean, maybe that's how they do it. They find a smaller college town, get some of their men on the police force to keep an eye out for any leaks, make an offer to the dean of admissions or someone higher up the ladder to hand over the information, and go from there. If I stay involved, if I see this through to the end, I can sleep well at night knowing I did what I could to get this information where it needed to go. Plus, the more people that know about it, the more flames they will have to extinguish, if it goes that way."

Alyssa and Emily both wore saddened faces that I couldn't convert.

"Look, I didn't ask for this. None of us did. I want to be back in Stanton with you guys. I wish we hadn't missed the party welcoming everyone back from our senior class. But Stephen's death—it's never sounded like an open and shut case from the beginning, to me, or to any of you. And now that we have a new lead, and new evidence, I mean—we may be able to save an innocent man."

Alyssa's painful look softened, but it was still present, even after she started nodding.

"I don't think Flores and Hannigan are terrorists, but once you review this information, who will you call?"

"I think Hannigan likes me more, so I'll call him."

They both agreed.

*****

We drove separately back to Ammon's apartment so Alyssa and Emily could load up their stuff in Alyssa's car. Ammon was there when we arrived and Emily talked to him about his family.

"Oh, they're doing really good. I'm sorry you can't meet them," Ammon said to Emily as he kissed her on the forehead.

"That's okay. Maybe next time they're in?" Emily asked.

"Certainly."

Emily and Alyssa needed to leave soon since it was a four-hour trip. Their parents didn't want them driving around in the dark, so they had to use whatever sunlight they could to get there. Emily disappeared into Ammon's room while Alyssa dragged her stuff around in the living room and packed it.

"Need a hand?" I asked.

"You should probably call your mom before you lose a hand," she replied.

"Oh, right."

My phone was reading about fifty percent battery, so definitely not enough to call my mom. Just kidding. Some people's parents are quite the talkers, but my mom seemed to keep to herself most of the time. And if there was a conversation, she kept it pretty brief. Not to make her sound unloving, I just believe she has enough on her mind all the time. Besides, she'd give me more time if I needed it. I knew that.

So, I dialed her up and pressed the Call button so we could start our long overdue conversation.

She answered, and I felt like I should have prepped myself a little more.

"So, son of mine, I think it'd be pretty hard to investigate a murder while your car battery is dead. Did you take a taxi everywhere?"

She didn't seem too mad, so I thought I'd be my classic self.

"No, us kids use Uber nowadays."

"Is that so? What the hell does that even have to do with cars?"

"I don't know. I'll look it up later and get back to you," I said. "So, who spilled the beans?"

"You know Chief Ramzorin wasn't going to keep this from me," she replied.

"Damn that old man."

"Jack."

"Oh, sorry."

Silence drifted between us and it made me think about what I could even say next.

"Y'know, I felt like you'd be a lot angrier," I said.

Alyssa looked over at me as if to say "Wow, you're setting yourself up for destruction, aren't you?"

"Yeah, I am mad. I wanted to see how long you'd keep the lie alive. Obviously, it's been three days and three nights. And yet, I have a feeling you're going to stay there still."

"I would escort Alyssa and Emily back, but…"

"That would be gentlemanly of you."

Hoping to not disappoint her, I said, "There's something telling me I have to stay out here; something saying that there's more to this story. But I don't know why it ever came up in the first place. Why something inside of me said I had to stay here and figure this case out myself. It's not that I don't trust the police, it's not that I don't have anything better to do, I…"

My mom's voice cut into me quietly but with such impact as she said, "I think I know why."

Huh?

"You do? Then, why?"

"Because it's what your father would have wanted."

Never had anything hit me so hard in my life. I felt an uncomfortable shock at first, but it was followed by a comfortable feeling of completeness.

She explained further, "Jack, when you started looking into Sam's death—I know Ben Whey was the one who suggested it—but you took the initiative. You decided it was best to look into it and you worked so hard to do so. Now, with Stephen—I mean, he was one of your father's best friends. And I'm sure if he was still here today, he would have been investigating all of this mess right alongside you. He loved you, Jack. I know you know that. But sometimes as time goes on, we forget what people felt for us while they were here. I never want you to forget how much your father loved you and how proud he was of you. I'm proud of you right now, besides all the bullshit you shoveled my way for the past few days. But you're determined, and you're a seeker of the truth and justice, just like your father. I'm so proud to know that this quality has passed on to you."

I stood near the front door with teary eyes and made sure Alyssa couldn't see my face. I'm sure my mom was the same as me on the other end of the phone. Not something I liked to think about, but that's just the way it was.

"Now, if you don't solve this case by the time you come back home, you're grounded," she said.

I laughed through the tears and wiped them away with my left sleeve.

"I love you, Mom."

"Love you too, Jack. Be careful."

The call ended on her side and I lowered my phone. It was not the outcome I was expecting, but it fueled my want for the truth even more.

"Did you get roasted?" Alyssa asked.

"Not entirely."

She smiled and added, "Do you need me to leave my laptop behind?"

"Yeah, that'd be good. And if you can write down your password for me."

"I already told you what it was," she said with a wink.

I laughed it off and went over to her for a hug. She didn't face me, so I hugged her from behind and kissed her neck. She laughed ever so lightly and tried to turn her head to give me a kiss back. I accepted it.

"Hey, hurry up, lovebirds," Emily said as she brought out her suitcases.

Before I knew it, the four of us were outside and we helped Alyssa and Emily load up their stuff into Alyssa's car. I didn't want them to go. I hated saying goodbye, but I knew it was only temporary. I'd be back there with them soon. Besides, with the video footage I now had and the fingerprints to turn in, there was no way it could take much longer to solve who the real killer was.

"Well, I guess it's that time," Ammon said.

Emily grabbed him and held him tight, so I looked to Alyssa and said, "We can't let them beat us."

Alyssa grabbed me and yanked me into her arms. We kissed a little more passionately than we should have, but I didn't care. Then, she put her mouth up to my ear and whispered those three words that we all desire to hear.

"I love you."

I was a little caught off guard, but I had no problem saying it back.

"I love you too, Alyssa. It'll all be okay."

She pulled her head back to look me deep in the eyes. I smiled back at her and she blushed.

"You owe me when you get back to Stanton," Alyssa said, and then she let me go and stepped over to the driver's door.

Emily and Ammon were still hugging and he told her it was time to go. She nodded softly and pulled away from him. He kissed her on the forehead and she climbed into the passenger seat.

"Be safe," I said through the open window.

"Yeah, don't worry. We will be."

I blew one last kiss to Alyssa and she smiled as she drove away. I turned to Ammon, who was staring off into the distance.

"Well, it's almost four o'clock. Will you be hungry anytime soon?" he asked.

"Sushi sounds kinda good. Would you be down for that?" I asked.

"Yeah, there's a place that can actually deliver here."

"That'd be perfect," I replied, but then I thought about the file folder in my car.

"Something wrong?"

"Oh, no, I just need to run an errand if that's alright."

"Of course. I'll be at the apartment so I'll let you in when you come back," Ammon said with a smile.

"Thanks, man, you're the best. And thanks for letting me stay here for a bit longer," I said.

"No problem at all. I just hope you can find what you're looking for."

"Yeah, same here," I said, and I made my way to the underground garage.

Chapter Twenty-One

The day was really escaping me as I drove over to the police station, hopefully for the last time. Not that I hated going there for some extra help, but I knew they were tired of me. And now that Alyssa and Emily were gone, I found it harder to stay focused on the task at hand. I wanted to watch that footage so badly, but I knew I had to do this first.

I was almost there when it occurred to me that I should probably call first.

"Hannigan here."

"Hi, this is...Sack Jampson, here with an anonymous tip."

He sighed loudly and said, "You got to be kidding me."

"Look, Hannigan, I feel like you kind of owe me. Y'know, after you embarrassed me in front of my friends."

"I thought one of them was more than a friend to you. That's what I could read, anyway."

"That's none of your business."

"Okay, Jack, I'm hanging up now."

"No, no, wait—I have something for you."

"It better be some chocolates or a bouquet of flowers for all the hard work we've done."

"Would you then just pass them off to your wife?"

He let out a slow breath through his nose and said, "I don't have a wife anymore."

"Oh, I'm sorry to hear that."

"It's okay. You can't really have a wife in this line of work. It's...it's too much. I couldn't give her enough love."

"So now you and Flores just accompany each other on lonely nights?" I asked.

"Okay, now I'm really hanging up the phone," Hannigan said with an angry tone.

"Hey! Okay! That was out of line, I'm sorry. You got to remember, I'm

123

nineteen."

"Yeah, well that's an adult in the eyes of the law, so start acting like one."

"Yes, sir. Now, do you want to know what I have?"

"Besides a smart ass and a lot of luck, what?"

"I have fingerprints."

"Yeah, I think most humans do."

"No, I mean, ones that I need analyzed."

I could hear Hannigan adjust in his chair and he asked, "How? Why?"

"I would just really appreciate it if you asked as few questions as possible."

"Jack," Hannigan started. "Why are you doing this? You know the arraignment is tomorrow, right?"

"Look, I'm almost at the front entrance, so if you could meet me outside, I'd greatly appreciate it."

"Fine."

CLICK!

*****

When I pulled up to the entrance Hannigan was just finishing up a cigarette. I smiled and waved, but he didn't exude the same level of excitement.

I rolled down my window and he ran up to me.

"Jesus Christ, Jack, if another officer saw you pull up to me with your window rolling down, they'd probably open fire on you."

"Well, I thought I'd make this quick since I annoyed you on the phone," I said, and I handed him the file folder.

He opened it up and glanced over the page.

"You used scotch tape?" he asked.

"Do I look like a professional?"

He shook his head and said, "It might be a little tough to read these, but we'll try. Can I ask what these pertain to or should I already know?"

"Oh, you should already know, Detective."

Hannigan shook his head again and said, "Okay, Jack, I'll have our lab man call you tonight if he finds something."

"Really? That fast?" I asked.

"He doesn't have much else going on, so I'm pretty sure it'll be tonight. Okay? Now, are you satisfied?"

I wore my dirtiest grin as I replied, "Not completely."

"Hmm, okay. Well if you're still in town tomorrow, how about I get you into the press conference? It'll be right after the arraignment. Is that enough for you?"

"Yeah, get me two passes. I'm sure Ammon would like to go, too," I said, and I drove off before I could push my luck any further.

*****

My mind seemed to be calm as I drove around the nice city of Eddington, but I still wondered what the outcome of the fingerprints would be. Hopefully, they wouldn't be a complete bust. Trying to be patient sucks.

I was really thirsty and couldn't wait to get back to Ammon's apartment. An Icee drink sounded delightful, so I stopped in a convenience store on the way back. It wasn't too bad a place, but the front windows were filled with random flyers about lost animals. That kind of detective work wasn't my calling.

The cashier greeted me and called me "Friend" as I entered and I said "Hi" back. Then, as I made my way over to the Icee machine, I felt the presence of someone behind me. When I turned around, I was thrown off.

"I thought that might be you," Mrs. Martin said.

"Oh, yes. Hello, Mrs. Martin."

She was dressed very sharp and her dark skin glowed in the fluorescent light, but her eyes seemed dull and hurt from all the events of the past few days.

"Shouldn't you be home?" she asked.

"How much do you know about me?" I replied.

"Stephen mentioned your father a few times, showed a photo to me and Derrick of the four of you together. You were a bit younger, though."

"Yeah, it would've been before my father's passing," I said.

A woman and her two younger kids walked past us and we made way for them in the aisle. The aisle we happened to be in had all the miscellaneous car knickknacks and gadgets, so I knew we wouldn't be interrupted too much.

"I'm sorry to hear about that happening. His sacrifice won't be forgotten."

I nodded to thank her for the sympathy. She ended up smiling and laughing to herself before saying, "Y'know, the detectives warned me that you might come bother me. They said you're a detective yourself."

"Did they really?" I asked.

She nodded and I laughed as well. She could grab anyone's attention from a mile away.

"I mean, maybe one day I'll be sworn in and everything, but for now..."

"Is there anything you'd like to ask me?"

Alicia Martin, even if she didn't mean to, gave off a very seductive vibe. I

125

didn't really notice it when I peeped into her house or saw her and her husband at the restaurant, but now it was apparent. It made me give Stephen the benefit of the doubt for who made the first move.

"Do you think Derrick killed Stephen?" I asked.

"Not at all," she said with a quiver in her lip.

"Yeah, that's what I think too. And I plan to expose the real killer, with the help of a Dr. Pepper Icee."

"This isn't something to joke about."

"I'm being dead serious, Mrs. Martin. I plan to get your husband free by tomorrow, hopefully."

"During the arraignment?"

"Yeah, I think that'll be a good time to do it," I replied.

She gave me a faint smile and said, "I agree."

"May I ask one more question?"

"Sure."

"Did Stephen mention having any enemies?"

She looked around for a second and I thought she was going to tell me something juicy. Instead, she said, "Yes, but never said any names or anything like that. Otherwise, I would have told that to the police."

"Did you not even mention the enemies' part when the police interrogated you?"

"No, I didn't think there was any use. Once they showed the search warrant and found the pistol, I felt it was pointless."

"But you still don't think he did it, right?"

"Of course not."

She sniffled and finally pulled a tissue from her purse. I stepped toward her a little more and said, "Hey, I'm going to prove your husband's innocence, okay? And then we'll all be able to move on."

Alicia nodded and said, "I believe you, Jack. Just don't disappoint me."

Chapter Twenty-Two

Late Monday Night

I wasn't really too adventurous when it came to eating sushi, so I stuck with a California Roll while Ammon ordered some kind of nigiri. We also shared an order of vegetable fried rice, which really sent me over the top, but Ammon also ordered some egg rolls and a miso soup for himself. After the Big Mac and fries, I wasn't sure how much I could really take, so I had to decline his offers for the extra egg roll.

"I really can't, Ammon, but I appreciate it," I said as I finished the last bite of the California roll.

"If you insist. These can warm up well in the toaster oven, so if you change your mind later..."

He stood up from the couch in the living room and stretched. Now that it was just me and him, he wore a black tank top with gray sweatpants. Not like I really cared too much or anything, but he was quite buff. His arm muscles moved around as he stretched and I heard him let out a sigh.

"Do you work out?" I asked.

"When I have time. Mostly here in my apartment, though."

"That's cool."

"Yeah. If you don't mind, that's actually what I was going to disappear off to my room to do. Unless I should bring my weights out here and you could join me?"

"Oh, no, that's okay. I have a few things I want to look over on Alyssa's laptop. I may be able to leave tomorrow if all goes well."

"Just let me know, and then I'll start my deep cleaning," Ammon said, and he disappeared into his room with the door closing behind him.

Well, we're not that dirty.

I took my plates over to the sink and rinsed them off. Unlike most apartments I had been in before, the hot water on his sinks seemed to get hot really fast. It made me think about how expensive this place was.

How did he say he afforded it again?

"My parents send me money from Egypt. Over there, it's not illegal for them to own a

whole city."

Must be nice.

I stepped back over to the couch and grabbed Alyssa's laptop. I was starting to feel tired, but the idea of seeing new footage made me excited. Still, I ended up stopping myself as I heard Chief Ramzorin's voice say, "Slow down, kid. Start from the beginning. Build the case up from the beginning."

Okay. Here we go.

Stephen Donahue was kind of a player. We can all agree on that. Yes, he did have sex with Derrick's wife, but I don't think that has to do with the murder at all. Instead, Stephen somehow got warped into the world of identity theft and started sending off files to some terrorist organization somewhere. He sent the emails to random Yahoo!, Gmail, and even AOL addresses that no longer exist. But, he left a trail of which files were scanned, because of that ticker machine.

Would Stephen really be that sloppy to leave that trail behind for anyone to find?

Considering the fact that his life was on the line, yes. I do believe based on the amount of money he was receiving, combined with the threat to his life, he may have blatantly made that mistake. So, he's scanning in the files and then… something happens. Something goes wrong. Based on the man I met, maybe Stephen didn't scan files on time or didn't want to anymore. Maybe they were going to make a hand-off system.

Who knows. But something went wrong, and then…

I pulled up the footage from in front of Stephen's office. I fast-forwarded to Derrick entering the front and going through the office doors. I rewound and played it again. And again. And…why not? How about one more time?

Derrick appears to be angry, blinded, y'know; the usual stuff when you find out your best friend banged your wife (using Alyssa's wording here), even if it is an open relationship. The point I'm trying to make is: he doesn't appear to be collected in any way. Clear?

So now we move on to when the next assailant appears. Derrick has had enough time to leave the premises, in my opinion, depending on where he parked. Or maybe, the second visitor saw Derrick go in and decided to wait outside, knowing that he couldn't get away with killing two men. Stephen was the target all along; that much was clear from the beginning.

Anyway, visitor two entered the office. I rewound and played his entrance again. And again. One more time.

The assailant moved quickly, like Derrick, but was definitely a man with a mission. He was standing up straight, the gun was tucked away in his jacket…

This wasn't his first time gunning down a man, and if I didn't stop him, it wouldn't be his last.

He kills Stephen after an extremely brief discussion and then walks out of the view of the camera. And we never see him again. Also, we can't tell exactly what he's wearing, besides the hoody, of course. But Derrick Martin was wearing a hoody as well.

I sighed loudly to myself. Both men dressed way too similar, and it annoyed me. Plus, with the cameras being a plain and grainy black and white, there wasn't much else to distinguish their features.

So with all of that being said, and with the idea of the assailant escaping through the window, it's time for me to watch the parking lot footage.

I fast forwarded to where I believed the assailant would be hopping out of the window. My eyes were instantly pleased by the high definition quality of this newer camera and the fact that it was in full color. And while it was dark outside in the video footage, the light poles in the parking lot made the video clear enough.

It was hard to see the catwalk, due to nature getting all up in its business, but I did see a black figure fall from the catwalk and make his way over to the parking lot. But when he got in his car, I could only see the black vehicle from the side.

So I don't even know the license plate or make and model of the vehicle he drove to the school? Dammit...

My phone started to buzz loudly on the table and I picked it up. It was a call from an unknown number, but I went ahead and answered. I noticed it was nearing 7 o'clock.

"Hello?" I started.

"Hello, this is Dr. Styphe from the lab over here at the EPD."

The woman had a very quiet and controlled voice. I felt like it was a tone that'd be used to speak to your friend during a funeral.

"Oh, yes. Hey, how are you?"

"Good. So, Jack, I was told to give you a call as soon as the fingerprint results came back."

"So you haven't even talked to Hannigan?" I asked, and I let the video of the parking lot continue to play. The police cars were arriving. The presumed killer's car hadn't moved.

"No, he said to call you directly. Are you ready to discuss the results?"

"As long as it doesn't paint me as the killer."

"I don't decide things like that."

Okay, not a joking around kind of gal.

"Yes, I'm ready."

The video continued to play. A few officers ran towards the school as the rest set up a perimeter and started making calls for an ambulance.

"Okay, well, we did have a partial print from you on the tape, since you administered the retrieval of the prints."

"As I told Hannigan, I'm not a professional."

"We know. The full prints that we found were mainly matched to a Tim Davidson."

"Okay, he's the janitor. That makes sense. Anyone else?"

"Yes, only one other person."

"Full prints or partial?"

"Full prints."

Maybe the killer wasn't so skilled after all. I glanced at the video again and saw that it was me, Alyssa, and Emily when we arrived at the scene. It was weird to see yourself on camera, especially a security camera. I noticed that I stood with my neck out a little farther than I would like.

"Who was it?" I asked.

But before she said it, everything clicked when I saw him walk up to our clueless trio from the vehicle that never moved.

"They match Ammon Samara."

I'll admit I had that brief second of doubt. That moment where someone tells you something you may not want to hear, so you stall. Your brain stalls. You don't want to accept the facts that are given to you, the hand you were dealt, the outcome of the roll of the dice. But there he was, in plain sight. It was Ammon Samara who killed Stephen Donahue. It was Ammon Samara who was not able to report back to the man who tried to kill me. Ammon Samara was the man we'd been looking for this whole time.

And as I looked up from the laptop, horrified beyond belief, I saw Ammon standing outside of his room staring right at me. My phone wasn't on speaker or anything, so I knew he couldn't hear what was said—or had he?

He put his hand beside his mouth and whispered, "Hey, Jack, sorry to bug you, but I forgot to turn my A/C on while I work out. You good?"

I nodded and gave him a "thumbs up." He smiled and nodded as he messed with the thermostat and disappeared back into his room.

"Jack, are you still there?" Dr. Styphe's voice cut in.

"Thankfully," I replied, as I started to close the computer.

The video kept playing and I watched as Ammon and I shook hands for the first time. A feeling of anger consumed me as I thought about the whole thing over and over again. I couldn't stop.

"Should I tell Hannigan now?" Dr. Styphe asked.

"No. Do you have a cell phone number for him, though?" I retorted.

"Sure. He did offer it if you needed it."

Sending Hannigan a text message wouldn't be the most professional thing for me to do, but it's all I felt comfortable with. Dr. Styphe read the number to me and I scribbled it down.

"Thank you, Dr. Styphe. I appreciate it."

I hung up the phone and closed out of everything I could on the laptop. My phone jumped out of the call screen and my thumbs jabbed into the screen as I made a text message for Hannigan. I sent: *I will reveal the real killer to you tomorrow at the press conference.*

I didn't have to wait long for a response. Hannigan replied: *We'll see about that, but I'll be prepared.*

That's when I heard Ammon's door open again. He wasn't trying to hide the fact that he was coming out, but I knew I'd have to act unafraid in the meantime.

"Jack, I am not thinking straight today," Ammon said. "Maybe that sushi wasn't the brain food I needed."

"It may have been counteracted by the miso soup and the egg rolls," I replied, trying to wear my normal Jack Sampson mask.

"Oh yeah, you're right. Anyway, I forgot to grab my water bottle."

"That is important when you're working out."

The sweaty Ammon walked into the kitchen and grabbed one from the counter. He kept his back to me as he asked, "Who was that on the phone?"

Lie now! Lie now!

"Alyssa," I said. "They're almost back."

"Hmm... I told Emily to call me when they were there," Ammon said.

Wrong lie, dammit!

"They switched who's driving. Alyssa was in the passenger seat and gave me a call. Emily was jamming out to music. They're both getting tired."

"Ah, our sweet girls."

You disgust me...

"Well, back to it," Ammon said.

As he started to walk away, I remembered the press passes that Hannigan had given me.

"Hey, I know you want to go to the arraignment in the morning, but do you want to go to the press conference with me as well? I got passes."

"That'd be good. I'd like to see what they have to say about Derrick Martin killing Stephen," Ammon replied without any hint of doubt in his voice before taking a drink from the water bottle.

And without giving away anything on my end, I replied, "Yeah, I'd like to see that too."

Chapter Twenty-Three

Tuesday

The Arraignment Hearing of Derrick Martin

It was safe to say I didn't sleep much at all last night. I kept waiting for Ammon to come out and suffocate me with one of the couch pillows, but the thought actually made me laugh. I mean, the pillows had little tassels on them. It would probably tickle if he did it.

Okay, I know I shouldn't joke about it. But I ended up texting Alyssa most of the night and revealing the information to her. I would have told her over the phone, but as I said with Hannigan, texting was the safest thing to do.

"Ammon? Really?" she texted.

"Yeah. I mean, that's where all the signs point."

"Poor Emily."

That was the understatement of the century. First, she dates Sam Miller and he ends up dead, and now she dates Ammon and he ends up being Stephen's killer?

God, give her a break.

"I'd like you to tell Chief Ramzorin as well. But maybe you shouldn't tell Emily right away. I don't want her lashing out at Ammon. Besides, I have to stay the night over here. I feel like if I leave now, he'll know something is up."

"Makes sense. But could you blame her if she did?"

"No, but that's not the point. I need more people to know about it, but I need to make sure they're the right people."

"What do you plan on doing?" Alyssa asked.

Texts can be so plain, but I knew Alyssa was probably scared out of her mind for me. As a good boyfriend, I had to reassure her.

"Nothing bad. Just pull up the local news here in Eddington tomorrow morning and watch online."

"I would, but my awesome boyfriend has my laptop," she replied.

I smiled. Of course, she could make me feel better in this shitty situation.

We wrapped up the conversation at some point with our "I love yous," but my night still didn't end. I was up, tossing and turning, thinking about it all over again. Why did I not see it was Ammon all along? He really knew how to manipulate the situation. I had a feeling he knew about the affair. I had a feeling that things didn't go his way, somehow…and he murdered Stephen for it.

I can't wait for you to rot in prison.

It was the last thought I could remember before my alarm started blaring at 8 a.m. The arraignment hearing was at nine. Ammon had finished up in the bathroom and I went on in to take a shower.

When I came out of the bathroom, Ammon passed me some warmed parathas and scrambled eggs. "I'm nervous, Jack," he said.

"Oh, thank you for breakfast," I said as I put the towel over my shoulders. "But why are you nervous?"

Ammon's face scrunched up. "I've never been to a criminal proceeding before."

"Yeah, well, this one shouldn't be too exciting with all the evidence they have on Derrick," I said. "He'll plead not guilty, the prosecutors will argue about their case, and that'll be it. And then a trial date will be set, I think."

"You know a lot about this," Ammon said. "A lot more than I do."

"You can learn a lot from cop shows. You just have to fact check them later on," I said.

Ammon raised his eyebrows at me and devoured everything on his plate. It was weird to think it'd be his last breakfast in his apartment. It could be my last breakfast if I wasn't careful.

"We'll need to leave soon, right?" Ammon asked as he rinsed his plate and stepped away to his room.

"Don't worry, I'm ready."

*****

After parking in the ridiculously huge parking lot, we made our way into the dark paneled and green carpeted courtroom. Outside, I had already seen the press setting up their cameras and sound systems in front of the small podium for the interviews following the arraignment. It would most likely just be the defense and the prosecution, in that order. I knew I'd have to make my speech somewhere in that time.

The majestic courthouse let our footsteps be heard by all those who wanted to. We weren't running, but the time was running short. It was only two minutes till nine.

But as we stepped in and saw most people were already sitting down or still chatting, I remembered that nothing starts on time, especially in court. The small memories I had from Billy's trial flew through my mind as I looked around the room. Alicia was leaning over talking to Derrick's attorney. Hannigan and Flores gave me a wave as they continued talking to the ADA. Lewis was already seated towards the front, but he turned and gave me a nod. Lois was there and I thought she was going to turn redder than the stop light outside. And then I guessed it was Derrick's family towards the front as well, along with other small-time reporters who wanted to make their newspaper articles as detailed as ever. Small towns always want the big news.

Ammon led the way to seats behind Derrick's lawyer and Alicia, which I found partly fitting and partly strange. Oh well. As long as he was nearby when I make the announcement.

Part of me wanted to do it during the arraignment, but I knew the judge wouldn't let that shit fly far at all. It had to be during the press conference.

Be patient...

As soon as we were seated, the bailiff came out and told everyone to start settling down. Alicia turned and looked at me, but I knew I couldn't give her too much of a reaction. Like, I couldn't just say, "Oh, by the way, here's the guy that really killed Stephen. Wanna get lunch after this?"

I gave her an extremely subtle nod and she returned one. Once everyone was seated and simmered down, Derrick Martin was escorted out in handcuffs by two other officers. I looked at Derrick and then gave a glance at Ammon. They both were about the same height, same stature, even almost the same skin color. But Derrick only seemed to carry himself well in a suit and tie. In this setting with an oversized orange jumpsuit, he appeared defeated.

He was seated next to his attorney and they both whispered to each other. Then the bailiff said, "All rise."

Everyone stood up. The judge stepped out and I noticed his name was Holderbee. Judge Holderbee. Why did that bother me so much?

"This is the arraignment hearing for Mr. Derrick Max Martin," said the bailiff, "and it is our only one today. Please, remain seated and quiet, or if you need to step out, flag down one of the officers by the front doors and they will be happy to escort you. The honorable Judge Holderbee resides."

Judge Holderbee looked like a judge, to say the least. His age showed wisdom and knowledge of the criminal justice system, and before he even talked, he seemed to be a fair and balanced man, as he should be.

"You may all be seated," Judge Holderbee said.

We all shuffled in our seats except Derrick, his attorney, and the ADA, who remained standing.

"Mr. Martin, you have been criminally charged with murder in the first degree against Stephen James Donahue. Mr. Phillips, how does your client plead?"

"Not guilty, your honor," Derrick's attorney replied.

"Your honor, this plea is a slap in the face to our judicial system," the ADA started, and I could tell he was going to be a hoot. "The fact of the matter is, Mr. Martin has made no effort to accept any offers I've placed on the table to admit his guilt. And this man is guilty. We found the murder weapon at his home, and we have videotape evidence from the university grounds that show Mr. Martin enter the office of Stephen Donahue, leave, and come back again with the murder weapon, while trying to disguise himself with a hoody."

Martin's attorney jumped to his fee. "My client was a dear friend of Stephen Donahue and would not harm that man or any other man on any given day. During his time in jail, he has repeated over and over that this is all a terrible nightmare. He misses his friend, and he has the right to plead not guilty if he so chooses."

"But even in his claims that he's not guilty, he refuses to point us in the right direction or give us any information as to why it's not him," the ADA shot back.

"I think that's what your detectives are supposed to do, Counselor," Derrick's attorney fired back.

Or me, I thought.

"They are here to serve and protect the people, which Hannigan and Flores have done wonderfully by getting this dangerous man off the street."

At last, Judge Holderbee decided to cut in.

"Gentlemen, please. If Mr. Martin wishes to plead not guilty to the murder of Stephen Donahue, that is his choice and his choice alone. Granted, we are all aware that if Mr. Martin is found guilty, he will face a minimum sentence of twenty years."

I was seeing Derrick Martin from behind, but I knew he had to be exhausted, mentally and physically.

"My client does understand that," Derrick's attorney said with a cleared throat.

"Alright, just so we're clear. Our first court date will be June 26 at 9 a.m. and we will go from there. I would like to ask that, after I dismiss, the defense and prosecution can speak to the media outside so that the people of

Eddington, and of the world, can know what kind of case we're dealing with. This arraignment is adjourned."

The gavel echoed brightly in the courtroom, and the murmuring resumed. Derrick Martin took a long look at Alicia and ended up walking away. His attorney seemed to make up for what Derrick had just done by leaning over and talking to her, but I worried about the future of their relationship. Maybe with the openness, this was bound to happen.

"Hey, Jack, come over here," Hannigan said.

I turned to Ammon and felt jarred by his expression. It was a satisfied smirk, plastered over his face. In his lie, he was happy that they had found the real killer. In truth, he was happy he got away with it.

Not for long…

I walked on over to Hannigan while Flores and the ADA continued talking next to him. Ammon didn't follow and actually started talking to Lewis as they met in the middle of the courtroom. I only caught the end of what Flores and the ADA were talking about, but it painted a clear enough picture.

"… and then we're going to hang him on a wall."

The ADA turned away from Flores and Hannigan introduced me.

"Henley, this is Jack Sampson. Jack, this is David Henley, our ADA."

"It's nice to meet you," I said.

"I could say the same, but I heard that it was possible you'd be over there with an attorney at some point," Henley replied.

"I mean…it was possible?"

Flores laughed at my answer and said, "It's all okay now. We're about to send Derrick off to prison and then Jack will be on his merry way."

"I actually don't find anything merry about this situation, so I'll just say, something like that," I replied.

Hannigan cleared his throat and I turned to see Derrick's attorney make his way out to the press.

"Statement time?" I asked.

I stepped over to Ammon and Lewis and said I was heading out to the interviews. Ammon followed beside me while Lewis stayed in the courtroom. He seemed under the weather, and I wondered if we had worn him out. Maybe he was worried about what might come of the video footage he had given to me the day before.

I guess we'll see here pretty soon.

We filed out of the courtroom and Hannigan explained that my pass could get me closer to the podium if I needed to be. There were folding chairs for the press. Most of them were already full, but there were two chairs together towards the front and I pointed them out to Ammon.

"I'm a little claustrophobic," Ammon said. "I'll stand back here, but you can sit up there."

"Okay," I said.

I sat up at the front and watched as Hannigan and Flores stepped to the side of the podium. There were cops everywhere. The cameras were rolling. But it wasn't showtime for me just yet.

My hearing was falling in and out. I was so nervous, so excited, and yet, so worried that I'd make a complete fool of myself. What if Ammon played it off? What if I ended up getting arrested for causing a scene?

But no, it had to be Ammon. It made sense.

"I'll take whatever questions you may have."

Derrick's attorney pointed at one man and said, "Yes, you?"

"Mike Polansky, *Channel Three News*. You say that…"

Is it possible it's not Ammon?

No, what am I talking about? He climbed into and came out of the exact same car. The car didn't move. He did not drive away at any point. He waited in his car and then came out to make it seem like he just got there.

But then… what about…

"Anybody else? Yes, you?"

No, Ammon thought all of this out. He framed Derrick Martin and then led the police to believe it was a stupid love triangle. He led me down that road, too, after looking through the tablet, but I was smart enough to take a different path.

"Okay, I think I've answered most of your questions. I'll let the ADA come up here."

He stole the tablet knowing that it had sensitive information on it. Little did he know, the messaging app was on there too. *Oh, Ammon, you really tried to make this play out in your favor, but I'll make sure it doesn't.*

"Henley, how about this case, huh? A crime of passion…"

I shook myself out of my dazed state and saw that the ADA was behind the podium. The press seemed to be in his favor with the whole thing, until one of them asked the question no one else was.

"Gloria Martinez, *Spanish News*. So, this is a pretty open and shut case then, right?"

"Uh, yes, Miss Martinez, you are correct," Henley said, just itching to run on to his next appointment or whatever the hell he was going to do.

I felt so many things: hate, anger, fear, excitement. I couldn't hold all these feelings in any longer. That's when I decided now was the time to step in.

"You know what, it's actually not that simple."

I stood up and all of the people in the press looked at me and almost all of them were annoyed.

"Uh, hey Jack, look…"

"Actually, Henley, could you let him speak?" Hannigan asked.

Henley and Flores gave Hannigan a look, but then Henley shrugged and said, "Okay, do whatever you want, kid."

Henley stepped away from the podium and I stepped up to it. To my dismay, I saw that most of the police officers had left with Derrick's attorney. Oh well, Hannigan, Flores, the bailiff, and two other officers were still present, along with the cameras rolling and the press hunting for answers.

"Hi, my name is Jack Sampson. Some of you may know me, most of you probably don't. But I will say that I know the truth behind Stephen Donahue's murder."

Everyone was extremely puzzled by me standing up there, even Ammon. I guess I expected him to run off as soon as I started talking.

"Let's start with a riddle. What do a small town in Pennsylvania, a private university in Rhode Island, and the university here in Eddington have in common? Any guesses? C'mon, you were all being so chatty before this, I thought you might have something? Okay, fine. They've all had a major problem with someone getting into their schools and convincing the upper administration to hand over student files with the intention of committing some serious identity theft. But who would want to do that? Who would want those files, you may ask? I've come up with a few theories, but hey, maybe we should just ask the murderer himself. Right, Ammon?"

As boldly as I could, I pointed out Ammon and the press all turned to him, along with the cameras. All the attention was on him, and he wasn't saying a thing, nor was his dark expression changing.

"Y'see, from everything that I've been able to gather, Ammon Samara is actually the man who killed Stephen Donahue, because…"

"… because he found out that I was sending off the student files to my brothers in Ramahk," Ammon said, with the location being heavily accented.

Now everything really made sense. I felt so relieved. Stephen wasn't the one sending off the files—he was the one who found out about it.

Ammon started to smile and laugh ever so softly. Hannigan seemed to reach for his pistol in his coat ever so slowly. The other officers around us also kept their hands by their guns.

"I always knew I'd love playing Jacks," Ammon said with the grin of a devil. "I know you think you're clever, Jack Sampson, but this is exactly how I wanted things to go. I wanted to be caught. I don't want Stephen Donahue stealing all of my credit for something I did. But yeah, I killed him. I killed your friend. How does that feel to finally hear it?"

The press was growing uneasy, but all cameras were on him, Ammon, *the killer.* The now confessed killer.

"It feels good admitting everything. Do you want to give it a try, Lewis?"

In a dramatic twist of my knowledge and understanding, Lewis stepped out from hugging a wall. He carried a TEC-9 machine pistol in his right hand. He lifted it up at all of us and said, "Nobody needs to move now, okay? Ammon and I are going to walk out of here. No one has to die."

Lewis' eyes locked with mine and I said, "Stephen, Alyssa, and Emily… they all trusted the two of you. You all were close."

And with such a low and hateful tone of voice, Ammon replied for him. "We were close enough."

Lewis was obviously rattled. He was shaking his gun like an earthquake was erupting inside of him. I knew he wasn't completely on Ammon's side, but he wasn't on my side, either.

Ammon turned to face the bailiff who had positioned himself behind him. He wasn't worried. He stared at the bailiff, whose hand hovered over his pistol and said, "Draw your weapon."

The bailiff stayed still and I glanced around to see if anyone had drawn yet. My great idea for making this our confrontation was starting to turn sour real fast.

Finally, the bailiff grabbed his pistol almost as fast as I could blink, but Ammon was faster. He did some move that he had probably practiced a million times, where he switched the pistol around into his own hands fired one deafening shot into each of the bailiff's legs. The bailiff's cry mingled with screams from the press as he fell to the marble floor. Blood ran down his legs. Ammon took a knee and grabbed the two extra ammunition clips from his belt, then turned back around to face me, this time, with the pistol.

"Nobody else move a muscle. I'm leaving now, okay? No one else has to get hurt."

"Why didn't you use that logic with Stephen?" I yelled.

"Don't you mean *we're* leaving?" Lewis asked with a whimper.

"Gentlemen, now you're just annoying me," Ammon said as he slowly walked backward. "Lewis, you gave up the one incriminating tape to Jack. Why? Feeling bad for your old friend?"

Lewis was horrified by Ammon's statement, knowing he was really alone. I had no idea what the man was going to do now to prove himself to Ammon, but everything inside of me wished I wasn't so helpless in it all.

"Surrender now and we can all stay alive today," Hannigan said, interrupting the exchange.

"Yes, but what is life without freedom?" Ammon sneered.

Ammon lifted his gun for a split second, parallel to the side of his head, and Lewis seemed a little distracted. Hannigan took the opportunity. He ripped his pistol from under his arm and aimed at Ammon. But Lewis wasn't as distracted as we had hoped. He fired a quick burst that flashed red over the right side of Hannigan's torso. The detective fell back, but Lewis didn't continue firing.

When he saw that Ammon started running scared as soon as he fired on Hannigan, Lewis froze. It was a lethal decision. Flores now had her pistol drawn and she unloaded on Lewis, who fell to the ground in a bloody mess.

Press scattered and screamed like a rollercoaster had come off the rails. As soon as I had my opening, I jumped out from behind the podium, grabbed the TEC-9 off of the ground, and ran after Ammon.

"Jack, goddammit!" Flores yelled after me.

I didn't mean to ignore her, but I was on the hunt. Did I plan on killing Ammon? No. But I felt safer with a weapon since, well, he had one.

He ran down the long hallway and appeared to try and exit through the front, but something stopped him. He fired and I heard more screams. I lifted the TEC-9, but knew it would spray way too much at this distance. There was no telling what I would have hit. Plus, I knew it'd be frowned upon if I made too much collateral damage chasing Ammon.

He finally arrived at the stairwell, but the door would not cooperate with him. I made sure I was behind one of the marble walls diagonal from him before I poked my head out and said, "Hey, Ammon!"

He looked over at me and fired the pistol twice. Marble debris burst out from the wall like a scene in *The Matrix* and I kept my head back. When I heard him rustle with the door again, I jumped out from beside the wall and fired off a burst of shots from the machine pistol. The kickback made me stop pulling the trigger and the bullets flung themselves into the wall next to Ammon. He scrambled to get the door fully open and then he jumped into the stairwell. I stepped out from the wall and glanced at the front entrance. Two other officers were down with gunshot wounds and my anger started to flow erratically. If Ammon wanted to run, then he should just run; not cause harm to innocent people.

I grabbed the metal door to the stairwell and yanked it open, but Ammon was right there ready to fire at me. Luckily, the door hinges were loose enough that I threw the door closed and the bullets hit it instead of me. Once the shooting stopped, I yanked the door back open and fired. He barely dodged the gunfire and I heard him bolt up the stairs, skipping two or three at a time.

Maybe I should have done the workout with Ammon to train for this shit.

I could only climb two steps at a time, but I heard Ammon keep running and running. The man was a powerhouse, I'd give him that. But I had no intention of stopping. We had to get him. Or I guess, by we, I mean, I had to.

I knew I could catch up to him, and he seemed too paranoid to try and exit on the other floors. He knew there would be too many cops. His only option was the roof.

But where the hell would he go from there?

After passing the door to the fourth floor, I heard Ammon struggling to open the door to the roof. It sounded like there was a padlock on it. I wanted to run up behind him if I could, but I knew it'd be too dangerous.

I jumped as he fired three or four times and then kicked the door forward. After I heard him run out onto the roof, I ran after him.

The sun was out in the east and I watched as Ammon ran across the gravel rooftop. I ran out after him but realized that he didn't plan on stopping once he reached the edge.

"Ammon! Stop!"

Ammon Samara did as I commanded and the gravel crunched under his feet. He stared out into the sun, and I could tell he was being transported to the other side of the world. To where he grew up and learned how to do all the terrible things he had done so far.

He was calm as he said, "I have a son, you know. He's still small. I've never seen him… He's over there."

"Well, maybe you should have thought about that before you did all of this," I said.

Ammon turned away from the rising sun to face me and said, "You're right. But, if I didn't do this, there would be no guarantees that my brothers back home would continue watching my son in my absence."

"That's why you did this? Because they threatened you? They forced you?" I asked.

"No. I took an oath, Jack. That this is what I would do for my brothers and sisters, because I denied too many of the jobs thrown my way. Don't you see? Men like me, where I grew up, we don't have a future. Your country either comes over and bombs our futures away or we set our own futures."

"I don't need to hear this shit. My dad died fighting assholes like you overseas. You're not going to gain my sympathy after what you've done."

There was the faint sound of a helicopter closing in on our position and I saw Ammon smile.

"It's almost over for me, Jack. You shouldn't have chased me up here."

"Did you really think you were going to get away with this?" I asked.

I tried so hard not to let my eyes dart over to her, but Flores had finally made her way up to the roof and had a black tactical shotgun at the ready behind Ammon.

"I did. But, I should have listened to Emily's story, about you being the kid who solved the small-town mystery. Never knew you'd get so involved with this one, but I guess I was wrong."

"Yeah, I guess so."

Flores made her steps very carefully as she got closer and closer to Ammon. She was still a ways away from him, so I knew I needed to drag out the conversation more, if I could.

"So, what are you going to do now? Blow your own head off? Jump off the ledge?" I asked.

Ammon smiled and shook his head.

"No, Jack. Out of all the training I've received, there is one thing I was told over and over again."

"And what would that be?" I asked as the helicopter grew louder.

"Make sure you kill the last man who crosses you."

My entire body froze as I watched him raise the pistol at me. I had the machine pistol aimed at him as well, but I knew shooting it would be fatal. Plus, I had hope that Flores would save me.

She fired the shotgun once right at Ammon's left rib cage and he turned into a puppet being pulled across the stage. With a sharp exhale, I dropped the machine pistol immediately after Flores fired and watched as Ammon grunted in pain. I did a double-take, expecting there to be blood all over the roof where he once stood. But, instead, Flores used the shotgun strap to slide it behind her. Afterwards, she stepped over to Ammon with the cuffs out and she said, "They're just bean bags. Still hurt like hell, but he's going to live."

"And Hannigan?" I asked.

Ammon continued groaning, and it only got worse when Flores dug her knee into his back to slap the handcuffs on. Finally, she looked up at me and winced as the sun tried to pierce her eyes. She explained, "He wore a vest, but a few bullets did poke through. That TEC-9 is definitely not street legal."

So there we stood. Well, Flores and I were standing while she kept her boot on Ammon's back. Ammon Samara attempted to move around, but she shut that down really quick. Now, multiple helicopters hovered over us to make sure everything was alright, and more police officers finally reached the roof with their guns raised. With the wave of her hand, they came to haul Ammon away as Flores and I remained on the rooftop. I stared off into the same sun that Ammon had, but only for a few seconds. It's really bad for your eyes if you do it for too long.

"What are you thinking, Jack?" Flores asked.

Well, there were lots of things. I thought about how Derrick could be a free man once again. I thought about how Ammon was now in custody. I thought about how my friends were safe back in Stanton.

So, with a smile, I turned to her and said, "I think it's time for me to go home."

Chapter Twenty-Four

Stanton, Michigan

One Week Later...

The doorbell kept ringing downstairs and I cursed myself for playing a new video game way too long. I was practically ready to go, but I wasn't at the greatest save point.

"Jack, c'mon! Quit...you-ing around!"

"Good one, Mom!" I called back.

I went ahead and saved the game where I was and turned everything off. My knee popped as I got out of bed and slipped on my Vans.

Tonight was the new date of the party Mr. Saitov was trying to have at the beginning of summer when we were stuck out in Eddington. Yes, I admit it was my fault that we didn't make it there on time, but oh well. At least I helped them find the right guy.

Stephen's funeral was the day after I left. I thought about staying, delivering a eulogy, y'know, all of that stuff, but I didn't think it would be fair that Alyssa and Emily wouldn't be able to be there. And don't worry, us young'uns aren't dumb enough to use Skype for funerals...though I kind of wonder if someone's done that already. I wouldn't doubt it.

But yeah, I finally came home and was given a warm reception. Sam's parents, my mom, and Alyssa and Emily all greeted me with plenty of hugs and praise. It was painful to see Emily, but she already seemed to be adjusting to the idea that it was Ammon all along. And then, of course, the chief was proud of me.

"Goddamn, Jack. I hate to talk like that, but you make me proud, kid."

"Thank you so much, Chief."

And now tonight, at Mr. Saitov's bowling alley, I was probably going to hear all of it again. But I didn't want to focus on the case, or on Sam's death, or any of that. I wanted to focus on all of our futures and how we all have different goals and dreams in life. I shouldn't be the only one that my town is proud of. We, meaning me and my graduating class, we are going to go on to do great things. Solving two murders before I had received my degree, that was nothing compared to what I planned to do in the future, and what my fellow classmates planned on doing in theirs.

Okay, enough with the speeches. I was ready to go to the bowling alley.

I ran down the stairs and my mom stood at the front door—with the absolutely all around amazing Alyssa Jackson.

But, the last sentence I heard my mom say was disconcerting.

"… yeah, Jack's always had a problem with that."

"Uh…"

"Speak of the devil," Alyssa said with a smile.

"If what you two were talking about had anything to do with bathtubs," I started.

Instead of making their faces red, mine turned red and the three of us started laughing.

"Get on out of here, Jack," my mom said.

"Okay, love you," I replied.

Alyssa led the way out to her car and I followed. My mom waved one last time and closed the door to our house.

"So, why did you decide to drive us to the party?" I asked Alyssa.

"I don't know. I thought it could be like when we first officially met? Remember?"

"Of course I do," I replied.

We climbed into her car and I gave her a ferocious kiss. She let it happen and went along with it, but when she pulled away, she said, "Jack, calm down. We have a party to go to."

"Are we supposed to be professional at parties?" I asked.

"It wouldn't hurt."

Alyssa pulled away from my front yard and I started to think back on all the years my family had lived there, all of the memories. It made me wonder what life would be like with Alyssa in the future.

Whoa, okay, I'll slow down. Don't want to think too much about that now, do we?

Alyssa reached over her right hand and I grabbed it. I loved her. I loved her so much. Wait, didn't I just say I wouldn't talk about this?

The sun was leaving the sky for the day and the clouds were rolling in. At one stop light, Alyssa kissed me and I kissed her back.

"Jack," Alyssa said, and her dreamy eyes looked all over my body. "There is one thing that I really, really wanted to tell you."

I smiled.

"Yeah, and what would that be?"

"Surprise!!!"

"Jesus!"

I screamed as Emily popped up in the backseat. They both started laughing so hard while I continued to shake in my seat. Alyssa said "Awwww," and Emily said, "C'mon, Jack, chill out."

"You've been back there the whole time!?" I asked.

"Yeah, duh."

"Dear God, you scared me."

Emily grabbed my shoulder and said, "It's all going to be okay."

Alyssa pulled over into the parking lot of the bowling alley and my heart rate was still trying to normalize. Emily let out one last laugh and when Alyssa found a space in the packed parking lot, they started to climb out. I was about to join them, but then my phone started ringing.

"Can't you tell everyone you know to leave you alone for one night?" Alyssa asked.

"I would, but…" I started, and I checked my phone. "It's Flores."

"Don't let her chat you up," Alyssa said. "You're mine."

"Oh, you know I won't, sugar pie honey bunch."

Alyssa started singing the classic to herself and Emily gave her a weird look. They closed the doors to the car and I answered the phone.

"Junior Detective Jack Sampson speaking."

"Hey, Jack, glad you answered."

"What's up?"

"I thought maybe after all the effort you put into this case, you'd want an update."

"Oh, well yeah, that'd be nice."

"Well, Ammon Samara was willing to give us a lot of information. I mean, a lot. Luckily, Homeland Security and the FBI took him off our hands almost immediately. Just took them a little bit to get there, since there's not usually an immediate demand for them here in little old Eddington."

"But, he did admit to everything?"

"Yup. He followed Derrick Martin to the university, killed Stephen once Derrick left, planted the weapon at Derrick's house… Oh, and before all of that, bribed Lewis into joining his cause. Made him screw all the cameras up."

"Dammit…"

"Did your friends have their doubts about him?"

"No, like I told you, Alyssa seemed excited to introduce him to me. But now…"

"Yeah, I understand."

"And the man who attacked you, he was found dead just outside of town. Ammon said that made sense since the man was supposed to kill Stephen, but he also never got to make contact with his bosses since you and the girls were around. And since you got away and knew so much…"

I couldn't think of anything else to say, and I saw Ben Whey waving wildly outside. I waved back to him, but then Flores started talking again.

"Jack, I just wanted to say, what you did for us—as much as it pissed me off when you first started, I'm glad you found out the true story behind everything. Now, Derrick Martin walks as a free man, as he should."

"Any word on their marriage?"

"I don't want to get in the middle of that."

I laughed and she laughed softly as well.

"So, how many more years of school do you have?"

"Are you trying to hire me?"

"Hannigan will be out for a while; I'm sure you'd be a good partner."

Alyssa's remark floated by my mind so I said, "I just finished my first year, so you may have to wait a while. But I did like Eddington."

"Damn, that's a shame."

The sun was setting outside and I wanted to go join my friends. But here I was, talking to a detective who was four hours away from me, about a case that was over. But in some ways, it was far from over.

"What about those kids? The ones whose identities were stolen?" I asked.

"I don't know for sure. The FBI is going to handle all of that. And look, Jack, I don't want you to think that Hannigan and I are bad detectives."

"I don't think that at all. Sometimes I wonder if maybe I hadn't been there, it would've eased the tension and you would've found the same info that I did."

"That's a nice thought. Well hey, Jack…"

She took a second to catch her breath as she said, "If you can't come out here to work, then in the meantime, are you going to solve any other cases?"

We both laughed about it. Sure, it was a dumb concept that I would run around and keep solving mysteries before I even finished college or got any kind of licensing. But since it had already happened twice, I took a deep breath, smiled, and said, "We'll see about that."

The End.

About the Author

Henry Cline was born in 1994 in Oklahoma City, Oklahoma. He has been writing since he was seven and started writing novels at the age of eleven. His other passions include playing the electric guitar, cooking, and baking. His first album, *Resilience*, was released September of 2016, and *The Platinum Briefcase* (2017) was his first novel picked up by a publishing company, followed by *Too Close for Comfort* in Spring 2018. *Close Enough* is the second book to feature lead character Jack Sampson. More books are on the way!